FEVER DOGS

FEVER DOGS

Stories

KIM O'NEIL

TRIQUARTERLY BOOKS
NORTHWESTERN UNIVERSITY PRESS
EVANSTON, ILLINOIS

TriQuarterly Books
Northwestern University Press
www.nupress.northwestern.edu

"Blue Baby" was first published in *Faultline*; "Dicky Lucy" was first
published in *Packingtown Review*; and "How People Live Here" first
appeared, in slightly different form, in *Orange Coast Review*.

Printed in the United States of America

10 9 8 7 6 5 4 3 2 1

Author's note: Inspired in part by the life of my mother, *Fever Dogs* is
nonetheless a work of fiction. Names, characters, places, and events are the
product of my imagination or are used fictitiously and do not represent actual
people, places, and events.

Library of Congress Cataloging-in-Publication Data

Names: O'Neil, Kim, author.
Title: Fever dogs : stories / Kim O'Neil.
Description: Evanston, Illinois : TriQuarterly Books/Northwestern
    University Press, 2017.
Identifiers: LCCN 2017006045 | ISBN 9780810135499 (pbk. : alk. paper) |
    ISBN 9780810135505 (e-book)
Subjects: LCSH: Mothers and daughters—Fiction.
Classification: LCC PS3615.N4354 F48 2017 | DDC 813.6—dc23
LC record available at https://lccn.loc.gov/2017006045

Of and for my mother

CONTENTS

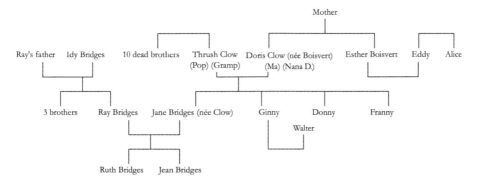

Mother

Ray's father   Idy Bridges   10 dead brothers   Thrush Clow   Doris Clow (née Boisvert)   Esther Boisvert   Eddy   Alice
                                                    (Pop) (Gramp)   (Ma) (Nana D.)

3 brothers   Ray Bridges   Jane Bridges (née Clow)   Ginny   Donny   Franny

Walter

Ruth Bridges   Jean Bridges

1

HOW TO DRAW FROM LIFE

→‣ Watertown, 2000 ◂←

THE WINTER BEFORE THE ANIMATION STUDIO IS SOLD, IT GETS A
Ping-Pong table. Jean gets the five-word job title no one keeps
straight, everyone gets edible business cards, bubble or mint, and
because the green light for season three is forthcoming, they get a
life model, Dragos.

Dragos is the Transylvanian temp. Not theirs. He works for the
neighbors upstairs, doing something for those suit people. But when
the sun drops, suits cannot keep him. At four, the sun comes level
with mulch. It makes the basement studio a woodcut hell. Fifty mon-
itors blaze, animation falters, and in the doorway is Dragos, nipples
rowdy with hair. Ping-Pong calls to him. He prefers to take the call
shirtless. All his preferences are unequivocal. He can speak English,
but prefers not to. Does he prefer Romanian? Hungarian? German?
He does not. What he prefers is nudity, and so it is arranged: every
Friday, for fifty in cash, Dragos descends, from his office to theirs,
arriving witchily with nothing but a robe and broomstick. None of
them care for that stick. *I* care for it, he says. He pitches the robe at
their heads and holds the stick on the diagonal in poses of glorious

1

defeat, the striker stricken, a story too broad for their taste, and they draw him. He has a scar across his lumbar. When he flexes, it grins. He has biker's calves and potter's hands and hair where you would not expect. Pose over, he circulates the easels, biting a boiled egg produced from where? *Point!* he cries, or *foul!* He corrects their work in ballpoint, adding scars and hairs omitted. Feet slapping concrete, all articles aswing. If you hide your work from his pen, he tut-tuts. My preference, he says. Show, I want to see.

That winter they are trying hard to have fun. They are on the brink of calamity. They mark time by deadlines and make frames move: storyboard, model sheet, animate, lip-synch. The stiller you sit, the more minutes you make. A minute of animation per week is a good rate, competitive. Jean is good at animating, not sitting. She is good at rate problems and can do Wade's schedules for him. She can help Wade until he gets a boss who notices all that he does not do.

At night Jean dreams of graphics software selection tools. Everyone dear to her laid out on a lawn and only key commands to save them from an oncoming storm. With the magic wand she tries to select her parents by color. They keep turning green, merging with lawn. When she narrows the tolerance, she grabs only pieces—her father's cheek, her mother's leg. She wakes up knowing always that she has failed to save them.

The men think of themselves as boys, and why not? It is a new millennium in the United States, just another year that asks little of them: cartoons for a living, contraception, no draft. That winter is the coldest in their adult lives.

On her breaks, Jean knits hats for the babies of friends. Her gauge is off and the hats come out big. As she foresees, her team wears them.

Saturdays Jean sees the dog of her father.

Ray, not a dog person, not a domestic person, lives alone with the former family dog in the former family house. When Jean and Ruth were in high school, their mother let them adopt Harvey from a shelter in spite of Ray's misgivings. The girls and Jane spoiled Harvey for three years straight. Ruth graduated, moved, then Jean. Then Jane left shortly after for good. Landlords would not allow Harvey. Jane had grown allergic to his coat.

Only Ray and Harvey remain.

The house is too much for two. The roommates claim outposts and keep polite distance. The rest becomes a half-struck set. Ray does not replace the furniture Jane took at his urging because he does not see it missing. None of us see what is missing in our homes. Only guests see. Our pathology spelled out in junk drawers. Our house our personal diagnostic manual.

Ray's dining room holds nothing but a milk crate of empties. The living room is a still life, Footstool with Circulars.

Where Ray lives and dines and sleeps is a concussed lounge chair in the den with a portable television tuned to any game, any sport. Here he eats big skirt steaks fried in a pan and white bread folded over fat slabs of butter—what Ruth calls Dad Seducing Himself. Two laundry baskets do for a dresser. In a self-styled sobriety of generous loopholes, Ray has sworn off beer for bulk wine from a membership warehouse club. He dispenses it in what Ruth calls Bridges Pours that hazard the brim, escorts each with measured steps to the chair.

What do Ray and Jean speak of?

Nostalgically, Jean asks Ray to draw the forces acting on wheels of different diameters racing in opposite directions down a hill. She sought his help with physics in high school in large part to watch him draw. Ray's handwriting is better than any Jean could conceive: rectilinear and forthright. He draws a beautiful arrow.

Jean copies, but to ill effect. Ray is, without effort or training, a fundamentally good draftsman as Jean, notwithstanding eighty hours a week at her tablet, is not. She loved her art teacher in grade and high school; she drew competently if she worked disproportionately; her career is not choice so much as the errant mating of worship and grotesque work ethic. It has taught her that she is uninterested in all aspects of animation but character. And to the degree our hand reveals our character—and if Jean holds any faith, it is this—Ray's signature is his manifesto. His print is his code. Why speak at all when you can print like that?

Also cars. They speak of cars. Is hers running smoothly?

It is.

Sometimes Ray proposes an outing. Want to go for a ride? he says. The membership warehouse club is a place where Ray takes singular pleasure in treating. If you want, pick yourself out something, he says. Jean wants very much to grant him this, but paralyzed by choice—five-hundred-count flossers, olives by the gallon—chokes. I'm not sure what I need, she says. At the concessions past checkout, Ray indicates the menu board. Have you had one of their sundaes? he says. They're awfully good. Jean orders two. They take a booth and across a sticky table, hemmed in by coats, consume methodically in silence what looks to be a gallon of soft serve between them.

Harvey's outpost, like Ray's, is chosen for its view. He holds vigil on the entrance-hall window seat, awaiting the return of faithless women.

More naturally verbal, Harvey requires more society than Ray. Those friendly to people remark how person-like he is. Harvey is so personable, they say. He prefers to drink his water from a freshly poured glass, spooning it up from a paw. He prefers to sleep with his head on a pillow or shoulder. He indulges in spooning. He wants his face touched. Also his belly. He loiters in high-traffic areas on his back, just in case. He likes pets and sometimes keeps one, a stray ginger who freelances as lap cat with several homes on the block when the weather is wet and hunts squirrel psychopathically when the weather is dry.

Harvey has a keen sense of propriety in matters of the bathroom. If on walks you stand too close with the poop bag while he transacts business, he stares dead ahead, not knowing you, his posture assuming a hyperrectitude that Ruth calls Thinking of the Queen.

But one weekend, Jean notes a runner displaced. Beneath it she finds an archipelago of pee. Did you move the rug? she asks Ray.

He didn't.

Once, she comes upon Harvey, head in toilet, gulping. He comes up for air and, seeing Jean, shrinks.

That winter it drops to thirty below. The wind blows sideways, so you fight to stand still. Animators arrive at work mummified and late. In thigh-length down they look like couches walking. Still, Wade and Jean run the river. Every day at five. It is how to survive the cube, where hours reduce to seconds. Put time back in the body.

It is dark. The paths unplowed, the ice molten. The river is not smooth, not skateable, but coagulate with floes. What Jean wants and misses is frictionless forward motion down a natural body of water that goes somewhere without end.

Not circles on a pond.

Not a rink.

At the Eliot Bridge, Wade says, What am I going to do?

At the JFK bridge: I can't marry her.

At the footbridge, where they cross over: I'm getting married.

They have to overtake whomever they come upon. Like every required thing, it is not spoken of, and Jean splits her side with pain trying. She is not naturally quick.

Good pace, says Wade, the danger passed.

Dragos speaks in piercing, incidentally upsetting insights about your character. He speaks at a lag, as if far-off by phone. He sneaks up behind you shirtlessly and squeezes your shoulders to solicit Ping-Pong, and as he squeezes, he tells you about yourself. Some of them like this, endure the insight for the massage—the unmarried mostly. It is free and helps blood flow.

Who could not like Dragos?

Cesar can.

Cesar hates Dragos.

That fag, Cesar says. Someone keep that Igor fag out of my office!

Other than Wade and Jean, only Cesar has an office, but it overheats with his Avid, and he leaves the door ajar. He takes frequent editing breaks to fuss with his pet project, a video montage of his life composed for the instruction and mortification of ex-girlfriends who have left him. Jump cuts of Cesar doing foeless martial arts in parks. Wide shots of him astride mountains baring teeth in violent smiles. Posed by all the best walls: the Berlin, the Great, the Wailing. Always in profile, as if these women might forget the mean close-set of his eyes. The sound track is techno. It is top secret, the project, but the techno is loud and the door ajar, and who has not seen clips? You have to go tell him when fixes are in. What's that called? you ask. Doesn't anyone knock! he yells, then keeps you twenty minutes showing off his plasma wipes.

Unknown to Cesar, his project does have a name. The animators call it My Life Is Great.

Cesar has a black belt he can find no good use for. At the Friday parties, he can be seen on the far side of the Ping-Pong table kicking the air around the head of some animator who pays no mind but attends serenely to a private store of nachos.

To Cesar, Dragos says, You are an angry sentimental man. Perhaps—how do you say it? Sadist, yes?

To Wade, Dragos says, You are like a father to me, although Wade is five years younger, terrified of aging, of balding, of fathering.

To Jean, Dragos says nothing, as if her presence were an error he lets go out of delicacy. As if he knows she wants judgment and, on principle, withholds.

Sundays Jean sees the dogs of her mother.

Jane's home is as small for its tenants as Ray's is big. There are never fewer than three dogs, hair, not fur, deaf, mute, cyclopic, dysplastic, syringomyelic—all rescues from mills where Amish rip out vocal cords with pliers to silence barkers—but if she had big acreage, money, and not a one-bedroom, there would be a horde. She ends every call, Got to let the dogs out. What Ruth calls Mom Controlling Her Exit.

At thirty, Jean finds herself converging with Jane just as Jane becomes most elusive. It is like one of those twins-separated-at-birth studies, but what separates is not space but time. They seem to be the same person, born of decades and families as different as one could invent, reunited in adulthood to find that they walk with precisely the same hyped-up stride wearing the same model of athletic sandal, consuming by the bagful the same ginger chew. The same trick shoulder. The same diagnosis: bad reading form.

On the nightstand, Hardy. On the VCR, Stanwyck. Inverted for months on the ledge of the tub, the same brand of shampoo with the same broken pump.

Sometimes Jane proposes an outing. They share a soft spot for the Hays Code. Want to catch a movie? she asks. They have a Hitchcock at the second-run. At theaters, Jane is a shameless smuggler. Throughout the film, at regular intervals, she pulls up from her purse fistfuls of contraband saltwater taffies. She holds them out tenderly to Jean in the dark.

What Jean knows of Jane, a private person, throws in with and breeds with what she invents. In her head is a shifty fictional biography. The primary sources are some dozen photographs, thirty-seven seconds of an 8-mm movie, no sound, and two failed interviews interrupted by five years.

Ruth says Jane had a baby sister who died.

Was preyed on by a father who drank.

Had a mother and older siblings who looked the other way.

By high school was homeless.

Had an aunt and uncle who wanted to adopt her, but the father, the drunk, opposed it.

Married Ray when pregnant with Ruth.

What do Jane and Jean speak of?

Jane's conversation is all dogs and cars and weather. The first is a topic of delight, the second, apprehension. The third is delight disguised as apprehension. Bad weather is, Jean thinks, a fetish. It beguiles Jane. It is one thing for which indisputably no one is to blame. To complain of weather is deeply seductive to Jane in a way she must deny to maintain the machinery of pleasure. How was the drive over with all that sleet? Jane asks with a wild glitter in her eye, hands wedged between thighs with a sort of repressed and gleeful fatalism. If you want Jean's mother to talk about herself, it is good to get her started with sleet. Traffic-imperiling is best. Inquire then about a dog.

After that, on cue, the dogs must go out.

Jane and Jean share this speech defect: they cannot speak to each other of the jobs or people that consume them. They cannot speak of anything past. It's a viral aphasia they contract from each other. That they do not speak of why they do not speak of what they don't speak of feeds it.

Without an origin story, what does Jean know?

What would Jean ask Jane if she could?

That winter the suit people come collecting old clothes for the halfway house in Union Square. They said it's so troubled boys can have a happy Christmas. Whatever you don't want, no stains or holes. Leave the bags on the landing and we'll bring them all over.

That's where my mom works, Jean tells Wade. Going on twenty years.

Wade says fuck sweaters. He draws Jean from her office and drives them straight to Daddy-O's, where they spend the day with Fenders. He and his brothers have a heavy metal band that changes names periodically but retains an umlaut. In the back of the store, Wade picks out "Hells Bells" and Bach until he finds the right guitar, the right amp, puts them on the company card, this their donation, its rightness a marvel. They leave the boxes on the landing. Then they run the long run.

As she runs, Jean recites French fables in her head, moral instruction starring foxes and bugs. The animal world gets hammered so humans can learn. The river shows the sky a broken version of itself. Trees on the path are missionaries from nature to teach Jean that she is dumb. She knows human anatomy but nothing about trees. Her tree knowledge is binary: there is the kind that gets naked in winter and there is the kind that does not.

At the JFK bridge, Wade says, Whoever buys us will run me out on a rail.

At the footbridge, Jean asks, A rail—what exactly does that mean?

They put you on a train and run after it, says Wade.

Throwing things?

Yes, loose change. Rice.

That sounds friendly.

It does but it's not.

Wade is faster but tires sooner. When his breathing labors at Eliot, where they cross back, Jean slows until he pulls ahead. The false surge gives him heart. This is what she hopes.

What is the point of Jean? At the airport once, on their way to that conference: Wade and Jean sat at the gate reading memoirs of arctic misadventure, noses lost to frostbite with neither regret nor purpose. For an hour they read, sucked lemon drops, compared cankers, only to learn minutes before takeoff that their gate had changed. Jean caught this. Jean caught things like this— weekly!

She gets the candy, the books, the true gate numbers.

Jean has no dog at all at home. Nary a fish nor hamster. At night: videos. Old ones. Young people then looked grown-up in their hats and hot-waved hair, spoke faster yet clearer like time was of the essence, communication key. There was no shame in sounding scripted. No ambition to look sixteen. These actors were young as she is now but quicker, and she adopts those she can as parents. Conscripts the rest as role models. What she craves is instruction.

For dinner, fake lasagna: jar sauce and cottage cheese. She eats it from a bowl on her lap. Rehangs the same pictures on the same walls with a level. How does she spend her money? On pretty curtains from France. They let in light and give no privacy. When she dresses, she crouches, crawling naked from bureau to closet. *La cigale et la fourmi*, sings Jean, who at work teaches herself what she can through headphones. She puts her faith in language CDs and renews them from the library in a timely fashion. Weeks of model sheets emulsify the brain. Nights of lip-synching turn whole lobes to porridge. She knows no one who speaks French and so she speaks it to herself.

The trick is passing time.

The trick is creating the illusion of time's passage by making each frame look almost but not exactly like that which precedes it.

Jean is a thorough professional.

Nolan, their audio editor, is Canadian and inspiring. Smart guy, smart dresser, father of three at twenty-six. A person can watch only so many videos, he explains.

Their days are dark and still with the small motor work of fooling the eye: faking three dimensions with two, motion with stills, consequence with sequence. The stiller you sit, the faster you fake, the more minutes you make. It helps to be sedentary. It helps to find the flicker of pixels sedative. Otherwise, refresh and frame rates can start to look slow. They can start to drive you mad. It helps, in the case of two, their prodigies, to have more than a touch of autism.

The boys keep the fluorescents off. Until four o'clock the basement is a cave. Inside noise-canceling headphones, they all listen to the same talk radio station Jean has never heard. Every now and then a guilty laugh erupts across twenty-five stations. Jean's headphones are the cheap kind. Only she hears the laugh. Only she misses the joke. She tries to imagine what it might be.

Dragos comes earlier. Three o'clock, two. He begins to beat the sun to them. His timing is off and he shows up during meetings.

At a storyboard crit, Jean solves all breaches of the 180 rule, and they are nearly done. No one likes a long meeting. She is saving changes when from the doorway comes the voice, vampirish and a bit behind the beat:

This storyboard, says Dragos. I saw what you showed. Effective, yes, but not *aff*ective.

Then, at a character meeting, they choose by consensus Hoffy's man-frog for the coach, a tyrannical extra, and are standing to stretch when again comes the voice:

This coach, yes, I get him, says Dragos. We all *get* him. But *you*. Ask yourselves. Why do you give so much power to the nation-state?

Dragos puts his hands on Hoffy's shoulders and squeezes.

It becomes a refrain. If anyone farts or hiccups or orders ham on rye, one of the boys without fail asks: Why do you give so much power to the nation-state?

Jean is using her left hand as a model for her right to draw and senses a spectator. She turns to find Dragos.

Why? he asks.

Jean looks at her hands. Why copy? she says. To get it right.

This is not your medium, Dragos says.

Pardon? Jean says.

Time happens, says Dragos. You think it doesn't, but it does. I see it happen and I see you hide.

Really, Dragos is not pleasant. In fact, he is a troll. That eggy diet—he smells like a volcano, does he know? That business of walking to work, an hour and a half each way, sweating, identifying trees with a field guide. A field guide! He comes by way of Roxbury, down the river, in January. Those are skeletons he is naming, and who has the time?

Idly, recreationally, Jean wishes for something bad to happen. She volunteers herself as victim in the wish. Behind the semen-smelling trees, perhaps, that place where the running path curves out of view. Something bad would be an exit. Time speeds up when things are good, slows when things are bad, a child can tell you that. The problem is that things get bad and slow, but never bad enough.

At home one midnight, Jean chokes on an apple. A piece of Granny Smith goes down wrong and sticks and she can feel its insoluble edges every time her throat seizes. She can breathe but barely. She cannot speak or swallow. She gets an old cottage cheese container and spits into that at ten-second intervals. What saliva factories we are, she thinks, with a calmness that impresses her. She checks what she is wearing—her mother's robe, patterned in seahorses, a link in the unbroken chain of seahorse-themed gifts from Ray to Jane the twenty years of their marriage, which Jane abandoned wholesale when she left and of which Ray asked Jean one weekend, Do you have any use for these?—and Jean decides to adopt a child. Perhaps a hard-to-place teen, though teens scare her. She knows a friend's infertile sister-in-law who did that, adopted four teenaged siblings, orphans from Russia. The irony was: she got pregnant right after. But the teens loved and doted on the baby—she had heard that, hadn't she? It had all worked out.

Jean pukes. It's over. The apple on the floor lies uselessly small.

They are at the airport, waiting to check in: Jean, Wade, and Cesar.

I'm so done with all this, says Wade. Fuck cartoons.

I for one would like to fuck time-based media, says Jean.

Let's arm wrestle! says Cesar.

We're not doing that, says Jean. Keep your hand, please. Why don't you read, where'd your porn go?

Only the insane read standing, says Cesar. That's a known fact. Wade, about this conference?

How much do I hate software? says Wade.

I gave you both just three vendors, I'll do the rest, says Jean. I made spreadsheets.

Wall-to-wall models, says Cesar. The models will be insane.

Who are we? says Jean. Which conference are we going to?

I could be a mechanic, says Wade. Formula One. Live in Montreal.

Me and two deadbeats, says Cesar.

Keep your hand, please, says Jean.

I am so on the wrong plane, says Wade. He speaks in a tiny fake voice: *Moi, je parlay français.*

La cigale et la fourmi, offers Jean. *La cigale, ayant chanté tout l'été, se trouva fort dépourvue quand la bise fut venue*—

Cesar says, I'm reading, do you mind?

Shit, says Wade. End-of-year evaluations. I was supposed to do yours, Jean. Write it for me on the plane?

When they get to the counter, the third ticket on file says Dragos, not Cesar. Barb booked the trip. Blessed Barb, their only admin, distracted single mother, collector of swizzle sticks—Barb was fond of Dragos. He had told her, You're not one of them, not long for here, and she took it as a compliment.

Dragos, who does not work for them.

Cesar is in a rage. He can break planks bare-handed. Where in God's name is a plank?

The hotel concierge is a small-featured man upstaged by his own mustache, which is precious and significant and complicates his talk cycle. He apologizes behind it: an error was made, naming names would not help (he was preemptively philosophical on this point), and as a result, their reservation did not exist, or did, but ineffectually. The rooms in question are taken. How the hotel wants to help them out, what it desires to do, is to offer as substitute with compliments the penthouse as yet unused by any conferee, a very special suite indeed, what is called the Honeymoon.

The Honeymoon is accessed by its own elevator. The elevator has a wrought-iron door that accordions shut. The elevator is from a horror movie, as is the hall it opens to. It is a long hall, symmetrical and doomed, awaiting its appointment with tidal waves of blood.

The suite's rooms are funnily grand. They assume a different-era person, someone better read, with plentiful friends and servants. They assume Jean's adopted parents, her old video clan. Hardcovers line a study, *Philology* on the spine, or James Fenimore Cooper. The upholstery is paisley. The furniture is what TV clients call aspirational. Every surface is cushy or glossy. There is a dining room with a high-gloss table seating twenty in cushy high-back chairs. A crystal chandelier overhead, its stillness affirmed in the lake of gloss below. A kitchen packed with superb knives. And in the living room, a grand piano. It shimmers. It shows them its backside, taut insides gleaming.

It, like the hall, has a swooning aspect. Everything perfect and primed for disaster.

You want to defile.

You want to etch your name in the table with the superb paring knife.

J ♥ W

You want to jump on the aspirationally cushy paisley with your dirty sneakers on.

Imagine if Dragos showed up, says Jean.

Imagine how mad Cesar would be, says Wade. It's just us, but can you imagine?

On New Year's Day, the studio is sold to a pack of New York publishing ladies. Their jewelry at wrist and neck is thick as rope.

What does happen: in malice, Cesar reschedules Dragos. He tells him to come that Thursday when he knows the publishing ladies will be there, prospecting what to own. On schedule, a loosely robed Dragos ambles in at four, props his broom in the corner, and lays his hands on the shoulders of their soon-to-be boss. You are joining us to draw me, good, he says. Welcome. Let me see you. You used to love art and now you love money?

Wade tells Dragos to go and not come back.

The ladies buy them but with conditions. Condition one: no Ping-Pong, no life models. Condition two: no piggybacking management. One person, one job.

Mom, can I get your advice?

One dog's tongue charmingly does not retract. It lolls out of its mouth on the toothless, eyeless side for a Janus effect, and Jane mists it with water to prevent it from drying. She sets down the spray bottle, chooses a comb from a basket of dog gear, and proceeds to study a paw.

Mom?

I'm just trying to get this road salt out. It gets embedded and burns the pads.

The vet says Harvey's in renal failure. He's pissing himself. He won't eat. They say there's nothing left to do.

Jane is combing the basket for tweezers.

Mom?

What does your father say? Jane's voice is barely audible.

Jean drags the Furminator a few times across her thigh.

He seems not to notice, she says.

Jane tweezers a granule and rubs in musher's wax.

Mom?

Jane says something too low for Jean to catch.

Mom, I can't hear you.

Jane says clearly, I think it's cruel.

That March, at the ladies' request, Wade attends a pricey seminar on how to manage time with the aid of a three-ring binder in leather or vinyl. The inserts are also pricey and filled with the maxims of industrious Americans. The binder people are openly mercenary and secretly evangelical, but Wade loves the planner. It goes everywhere with him. One day, he goes home without it. Jean finds it in the office kitchen. Tucked in the back is a multipage list. Five years of runs: minutes, miles, dates. His times and hers. With an asterisk, he notes all the times he thought she held back. The footnote to the asterisk says *fucking Jean lets me win.*

On their last run together, Jean keeps pace with Wade the whole way. When he goes faster, she speeds up. At Eliot, she passes him.

Back at the studio, Wade joins her, breathing hard. Jean, I have some bad news.

I'm fired, she says.

It's the new boss, he says. She says we do the same job.

After Wade dismisses Dragos, he goes upstairs to see him. It is, after all, a suit shop and Wade needs a suit.

Wedding or funeral? says Dragos. He is wearing a worsted-weight three-piece affair with high-powered cufflinks and sedate tie, and the sight of him like that fills Wade with dread.

I'm getting married, says Wade.

He undresses to boxers while Dragos waits. Wade has never been fitted for a suit.

Dragos measures him. The fitting is my gift to you, he says when Wade tries to pay.

Wade protests.

You have been like a father to me, says Dragos. And for future, I will say, it was not necessary to undress.

That spring Wade does marry. Very quickly does he father.

After consideration, as a wedding gift, Jean buys Wade a gift certificate to a video store that sells rather than rents. He likes to own all the movies he has seen, though it seems to her a poor investment.

Ruth flies in.

Jean holds the crate while Ruth sidelongs the window seat. It is Ruth who will lift Harvey for a last vet trip. But Harvey is not at his perch.

Dad, have you seen Harvey?

I haven't, Ray says from the den. He stands.

They call Harvey's name. They look behind doors. They scour the wastelands: the one-pan kitchen, the hangerless closets, the reservation of mug trees denuded of mugs.

They check the halls, checkered in Tinkle Turf.

Could he be upstairs? asks Ruth. Does Dad even heat up there?

Harvey barely moves, says Jean. He hasn't climbed stairs since we left.

Today, however, he has managed all sixteen steps to their parents' ex-bed, where he lies stiff on unused sheets, sacramentally centered, belly up and open for business. About him a wronged symmetry.

How long has he been waiting?

Neither Jean nor Ruth can decide a way to move.

We'll freeze to death standing in this room, Ruth says.

Jean's final day at the studio, she goes running alone. It is the last week of winter, negative ten with windchill and the sky densely white. The river lies blanketed. Beneath the JFK bridge, Jean quits the path. She plants a foot in ankle-deep snow onto ice she can't see. She steps away from the bank, to test what the ice can hold. Miles off is Eliot Bridge. Down the river she runs toward it.

When she returns to the studio lot, she cannot feel her nose or hands. Her blood has evacuated these disposables and repaired to her chest, favoring the organs. Everyone is shoveling out in a hurry. A whiteout is due. Roads will be closed in an hour.

Now or never, each boy tells her as he leaves.

There is a light on upstairs.

Dragos answers her knock in gray gabardine, double-breasted, with left breast pocket square, and the sight of him like that fills her with comfort.

It is better to quit than be fired, he says. He lifts pants at knee to sit. But either is good. A time to rejoice. Now you too are temporary.

May I ask a question? Jean asks.

You may ask dozens, he says. They will be of no consequence.

How will you get home? asks Jean.

Dragos closes his eyes and remains like that for so long that Jean must console herself with the sound of his breath.

I will stay, he says. I often do.

And what do you do? Jean asks. In your job.

Dragos waves at the walls of suits around him. I fit men into these. His eyes are still closed. Americans prefer play clothes, he says. They prefer to dress like children. As if every occasion is play occasion. What at home we wear to work, they wear only to funerals.

Dragos frowns. You have been to one recently. But dressed very terribly.

More or less, Jean says.

The story Jane likes to tell of Jean is this: when Ruth was three and Jean two, Ray brought home walkie-talkies from the lab. As a test, Jane took a handset to the five-and-dime down the block. Ray and the girls took turns speaking to Jane through its mate. Ray asked Jane if she would pick up razors. Ruth asked Jane if she would pick up pickles. When it came Jean's turn, she insisted Ray and Ruth leave the room. Here Jane reports a protracted silence on the line filled with the infant drama of mouth breathing. Finally came the question: Mom . . . are you real?

Jane's reply was to laugh.

Still the question plagues Jean.

Dragos opens his eyes and directs his speech to Jean's nose, which she can sense leaving the nest of her face, asserting its own distinct color and style.

Your face, he says. What have you done?

Wait, she says. One more. *Encore une question.*

For what wait? Dragos walks to the window. It is not me you want. Your questions in all languages are perfectly misdirected. As if knowledge is what is needed. Ha! Dragos raps the sill fast with his fist. You know enough. Now find a suitable place to put it. A sculpture, a book, or who knows, you rob banks. Which for the repressed?

Extended in his hand is a handkerchief.

Adopt me, thinks Jean. Or be adopted. Or together let's adopt some teens.

A book, Jean says.

With the handkerchief Dragos wipes clean a pane. He looks without fear at white on white.

how did your sister die?

2

BLUE BABY

→ Brighton, 1953 ←

JANIE RIDES A CAB IN A DRESS IN THE SNOW.

It is that dawn hour when the young sun pops and spews maraschino-red.

Out the window, red-gray Brighton's a smear.

Franny is a blue baby. Her heart has a hole. Sometimes it leaks blue blood into red. If this happens, you must rush to St. Anne's with a St. Anne's cab voucher and blood doctors will give her a blood transfusion.

Janie fake sneezes but Franny bucks.

Janie sings about the jelly pot but Franny goes screw-eyed.

Janie sings about the fissure in the moon and the outflow of cheese.

All Janie's songs entail food and Franny starts up again wailing, flat as a gull.

If anyone could see Janie in the cab in the dress in the snow they would say: She is rich. She is rich and stammers. Yes, she is eight and tongue-twisted but remarkable and nice, holding her baby sister like the child's own mother. Or else they will smell lice killer in her hair and expired milk on her breath, and say: She's a shame. Playing dress-up alone, she called the cab too late. Dressed up in that green dress, and look at that baby all blue all over. The driver has two moles on his neck substantial as turnips and would not come inside Fidelis Way Housing. *Fidelis Way Housing Block C*, Janie said clear on the phone. But the cab honked at Washington and would not budge. The man with the turnip neck said nothing when she gave him the voucher. Just held it to the end of his nose, then with undue ease released the clutch.

Janie's dress invites the looker to lick it. It is an ice cream green, a dotted Swiss. Pleating on the chest and organdy trim and Peter Pan collar and the petticoat slithers. It is the only gift Janie has ever received that did not leap from a Woolworth's bin into Uncle Eddy's magnetized hand. *There's really nothing to buy here, is there, Janie?* Every Sunday later on the streetcar the big hand opens and in it are things. The dress is not a hair ribbon and it is not a rubber donkey. It is not a gumball bloodshot and irised like an eye. The dress is the spring sky of Franny's face, but Franny struggles without sound and darkens.

Uncle Eddy gave Janie the dress. He gave and regave it and said, Don't tell. Hide it and save it for New Year's. Don't tell.

Uncle Eddy is a fly. He works high up. He builds building skeletons—he is a steelworker and a one-half Mohawk horseman. His hands are smart as Lassies, smell of Lava soap and lye. Holding his hand is like holding hands with a foot. What Janie would like is to do Eddy a favor he is not expecting and of which he never imagined her capable. She would like to win ten dollars at the trotters and shrug. Here, she'd say, I don't want it, you have it. Suppose she saved him from wasps. Say she cured him of warts. In the nick of time, she would like to remove his appendix.

If a cop said *which of you took this gum*, Janie would say, I did it, I took it, me.

Don't tell Donny, but Donny's at St. Anne's. He has been one year there in the TB ward. His very first tour, first time out of Brighton—Donny was excited and in his Navy duds clammy, and for his good-bye photo he stood on the roof of a car in a Donnyish way, a small person overachieving with posture—well, he served two months and came back coughing. In the Philippines, people empty piss buckets out windows, wipe their asses with their hands. That's what you get, said Pop. Go down a shithole and you find a whole bunch of shit.

When Pop was Donny's age and younger he ran rum out of Halifax and made his way giving soft Donnys the slip.

Now Donny lives inside a stand of screens and you have to speak to him through a black grill on the wall. The wall is hungry and the grill is its teeth. The voice buzzing through it is no one she knows. The voice scrabbles the air—hectic, maligned, frayed— *Janie? Is that you?*

Ginny says Donny is a reader of smut, but don't tell Donny.

Don't tell Ginny, but Ginny is in Stoneham. She has a husband and a tree. Its arms droop. A half-closed umbrella you can get inside. It is Ginny's tree, and if Ginny wants to she can hack it down with an ax. She can grind it into smithereens, manufacture toilet paper, and wipe herself with that for the rest of her life. Ginny is the cash prize winner of lookalike contests. She knows which way to tilt and to smile. *Tilt. Smile.* Her smile's a chummy blackmail. It has something on you but finds it amusing. The smile looked like Shirley Temple's, now it looks like Myrna Loy's. Ginny has a golf club that no one but her should touch because other people might

29

touch it wrong and crack the new credenza. Ginny has a golf club cozy that Janie knit. It started off as a Franny bootie but came out fat. Ginny cannot locate the cozy *this very minute*, it's somewhere, no doubt somewhere in a drawer. Ginny has a sort of girdle with removable ass pillows. It lives recklessly in a nightstand, third drawer down. No one should open the drawer but Ginny, but that doesn't stop Janie.

The pillow is satin.

It is the color of a tongue.

It tastes like hair.

The last time Janie saw Ginny was yesterday, Christmas.

Don't tell Ma or Pop.

But Pop is in jail. From bed, Janie heard Ma take the call and go.

Christmas at Ginny's, and the trouble was Pop. He'd pieced together a junk-parts car. Ma can't drive, can't read, can't write. She dictates to Janie her letters to Donny. She writes of two things: neighborhood bull dog sightings and small sums of money she's won at bingo (enclosed). When she wants to tell Esther secrets, she does it in their mangled girlhood French. Sometimes she thinks she's speaking French but is not.

Ma said to Pop, Thrush, you've had a lot. A cab's a lot, but we could use a voucher—and Pop said I can drive fine if you just shut up. Shut up yourself and shut up the baby and shut up the girl—though Janie had already ceased to whistle—shut up the world, my head's fit to burst. The car shimmied and heaved and Franny goat-cried in Ma's lap. Sock feet flailing on pencil shins. From the backseat Janie leaned forward to check Franny's cheeks: pink with two draining pools of red. Soon they'd be white if she didn't stop crying, and if she didn't stop then, they might go blue.

When Franny was born, she fell out backward. Ma was old to give birth, old now to mother. But out dropped Franny, and what Pop said to Janie was wrong: That is no child of mine and don't you say a word of what I say to no one.

Janie's mouth is a nozzle. Words, wrong ones, dash from it like bugs. To Franny she says, *our father fell off a ladder, our father lost his job, Pop fell asleep smoking and set his shirtsleeve on fire.*

When her heart doesn't leak, Franny is a baby supreme, wise, sleepy, quiet, sweet-breathed, chub-jointed, cabbage-leaf-eared, a champ. Her eyes track Janie, wide-set as a marmoset's and so wide open, like Janie's bewitched her, like Janie's a show.

But snow glued the wipers and Franny grabbed lungfuls and her heart got confused and mixed up colors and Pop said *mother of God, my head* and the car spasmed into the Olds at the yield. The Olds spun out into a guardrail. Onto the shoulder unfurled a tall priest. Six-three, called Ma, six-four, called Janie. They, short Clows, were all high-precision guessers of height. Short Pop abstained; he said not a word. He was one of eleven bounty-hunting brothers, orphans, the rest of them without mercy and tall. All of them died of the flu before twenty.

At twelve, for the first time, Pop found himself alone. He trapped lobster and distrusted the pious. He dreaded the charity of men, fake brothers who wanted to make you small, he ran rum. At seventeen he came ashore Boston, met Ma, and stayed. He painted houses, but painting was idiot-slow and indifferent to luck, and luck was Pop's distinction and gift. He liked a lucky win. His favorite win was the steal. Whatever came to him required no thanks. Picture a mustache, a heavy hand with pomade. A simmering wound-up short man's strut. He could dance the dances you win at, fox-trot, cha-cha, but when he failed to win them, he gave them up cold. He was five-five, married a four-ten preteen, had Ginny, Donny, Janie, and, too much later, Franny.

In boyhood Pop's trick was speed and knees.

The priest said, I forgive you, son, no harm done. But do you not know the meaning of *yield*?

Forgive was bad. *Son* was worse.

Pop said, Father, I'll teach you the meaning.

The priest must have had brothers too. He sidestepped the tackle. Janie heard from the car Pop's head crack the rail. Red leaked into white and the only good thing was that Franny stopped crying. Franny and the priest and the snow went pink. Pop exhumed his top part first. The priest wore a funny look while Pop cursed the snow. Ma said the man was probably on his way to a sermon. Making last-minute revisions maybe.

Janie in a dress on a hospital chair.

A nurse with ribbon candy: Such a pretty dress. Is it new?

Same nurse offering pillow mints and pens: Can't you write us her name? We need to call her mother.

Freckled nurse to first: No one answers the phone. Is there no one else to call?

Freckled nurse, crouching: She won't talk. Maybe she's deaf.

When Franny went still in the cab all Janie's words seized. They pinballed her throat. They fell stunned to her gut. You'd have to excise wet lengths of intestines to find them.

What she did, she wrote Franny's name in red and then Donny's.

When Ginny came to the door, she said right off, Your head! How awful, what a sight, does it hurt?

What Pop hated most was someone noting his losses.

He edged past her, saying, Ha! What kind of a thing is that?

Ginny's husband, Walt, had put up an imitation tree. The house bounced light. It smelled of lemon cleaning agents and all the chairs matched. On the mantel were decorative monkey-faced elves. Janie coveted the elves. And in a corner, the tree: floor-to-ceiling variety, fanatically conical, hung limb to limb with department-store balls. The balls wore little tutus. The tree had an incumbent swagger that reminded Janie of Pop.

There's Walter, said Pop. He gave Ginny his snow-pilled coat and stuck his hands in his pockets.

Some kind of accident? Walt went only by Walt. Can I get you some ice or something for that?

You can get me Scotch, no ice. That tree, said Pop, could use something, if you ask me. Looks like it's past due its watering.

It doesn't take water, said Ginny, plucking snow pills. She collected them neatly in one cupped hand. The beauty of it is that it stays nice forever, never wilts or needs water or drops quills on the floor. A good investment is how we see it.

Tough year, Walter, said Pop. I can sympathize. I imagine the kiddie porn business has its off years too. Take a tip from a union man. What you fellows need is organization.

Walt looked at Ginny, who was still holding the coats.

My word, said Ginny. Pop, you know perfectly well that Walt is employed as a photographer of quality high-fashion children's wear models. He's employed by Sears, Roebuck. He just finished their catalogue.

Sure he does, said Pop, them old days are bygones. Right, Walter? That's piss under the bridge and let's hear no mention of it. No, I won't hear it. My idea is this. You buy outright a high-tax piece of land like this, seems to me you owe yourself a good-smelling tree once a year. Any would do. I seen some in your yard put this sucker to shame.

Thrush, said Ma to Pop. Let Ginny put away the coats.

I'll take that drink outside, said Pop. Boiler trouble, Walter? Too much heat gives a person the sweats. I can see you both got a good sweat rash going. No end to your troubles. No end in sight, said Pop, finding the Scotch in the cabinet. Don't nobody know the troubles you've seen.

Aren't Esther and Eddy here yet? said Ma when Pop closed the back door.

Eddy and Esther were held up by snow.

Meantime, the house was ready and big. It was toured down to its last closet and shoe tree, and there was no part of it that was not ripe with education. Most ideas Ma held needed correction. There was the outer curtain and the inner curtain. There was the sofa and there were its rubberized shoes. There was the golf club and last year's cozy at large. There was the rug and its nonslip underrug. It was not clear what was being protected from what. Ma began walking on the balls of her feet. Janie toddled an elf at Franny in her bassinet and Ginny noted that that elf, all the elves, were in fact collectibles. Posable, true, but they *had been* posed. One pose per night was all they could bear.

When would Ma walk on her hands? Janie whispered. Was it time for her to light a match with her toes?

Third rounds got poured and nuts got shelled. Pop did not come in and no one missed him.

When Eddy and Esther arrived at last, everyone had their own private hoard of pecans and sat low-slung in matching chairs watching Franny snore.

Is this a séance? Esther said, facing Eddy. Why does everyone look in need of a prune?

Her dress was bare-backed with a pattern of badgers playing cards. Esther loved cards. She used to read tarot, fresh off the farm, a stringy teenager junk-jeweled in the Forest Club window. Esther and Ma claim Gypsy blood. Janie does too because she is Ma's child. Now Esther despises tarot. Her best game is poker or maybe blackjack. She always doubles down.

Everyone has to look like someone and it is Janie's long-range intention to look like Esther. Hound pretty, flagpole thin, truth-sniffing eyes. Earrings graze her clavicle. Alice says Esther dresses like a tart. She says Eddy left his wife and church to marry Esther and that God cannot, by law, forgive him. There are laws of forgiveness that all must abide. Alice knows about heaven and is planning to go there. Alice owns Patricia Shannon the pinto and four younger show horses, two mink coats, a hat piled with paste plums, and all the bingo halls and half the homes of Woonsocket, Rhode Island. A Coupe de Ville, white. When she drives downtown, she stops midintersection and a cop whose mortgage she holds trots up to park it. Have it back in an hour, says shopping Alice. A globular person with saddlebag arms and seagull legs and a grown-up daughter Belle who eats paper on the sly. Gravy-faced Belle, who cannot meet company, cannot tie her own shoes. Over the top of her corset Alice muffins out. In slacks: a big woman trying to climb out of a small one.

Don't tell Ma, Pop, Ginny, Donny, or Alice.

Only Esther and Eddy give gifts. But last Christmas, Aunt Alice sent a gift through Eddy. It was a girl made of china in a bonnet on a stump. The girl had blimp cheeks. Bumcheek cheeks. *What a likeness. This reminded me so of you!* said the note. *Please return the box.*

The girl moped from the dresser. Why do you look so funny, said Janie in bed, feeling her own nose. Looking at me funny. Little Miss Bumcheek. One day, she extended the girl pity and took her down and gave her Ma's leftover tea. The tea stained the cheeks brown. Janie washed the girl in the tub, but the soapy girl twisted from her hands in spite and off snapped the flowering twig from the stump. Last week, Alice sent back the same box, empty but for a note: *Please return the Apple Girl to me in this. I will see how well you care for nice things. If she is in good condition, I will send her back along with a lovely dress not for everyday wear. You may wear it when you see me on New Year's Eve.* My sister, Her Holiness, said Eddy when he read it. Never mind, Janie. You'll get your dress anyways and won't Alice have a fit.

Alice wouldn't come to Stoneham, and Janie said to Esther, Oh! I like your dress.

Esther extended her tongue, said: Aren't I awful? But wait till you see what Eddy got you.

Patricia Shannon had a good sulk when she saw me come in with the brush, said Eddy. *Where is my Janie*, she wanted to know. I promised we'd have you out there New Year's.

To Ma, Esther said, Where's Thrush at?

Pop was still outside and Ma said now was a good time.

For Franny, Janie opened the bib and blocks then opened her own gift and took out the dress.

Hold it up, said Esther. Didn't I say so? Eddy's got an eye.

Ma rubbed the material between an index and thumb. Too much, she said, smiling.

I got an idea, Janie, said Eddy. You wear that next week with me to see Aunt Alice.

I got an idea, said Pop. He had slipped in stealthily and stood behind them face immobile. A hotshot martyr drawn to be quartered and faking not to mind. He looked past Eddy and with an excess of delicacy removed the dried spittle edging his mouth. Here's my idea. You want to spoil kids, get some of your own.

Eddy said, Thrush. We thought you were off building an igloo.

Pop said, Janie, your uncle is a comedian.

Esther said, Isn't anyone hungry? I could eat my own shoe.

Ma sat blinking at carpet weave.

Pop said, I don't think you hear what I'm saying.

All right, Thrush. Eddy removed a thing from his eye. And what are you saying?

Pop said, I'm saying we don't accept. I'm saying my kids aren't orphans.

A third nurse says to the freckled, Did they find the mother? It's a shame, really awful, but you know, I almost can't feel bad for her under the circumstance. People like that I can't understand. Who I feel bad for is the mute, the sister.

Hush, will you, says the first. She's right there.

Janie pukes. Her green dress goes brown. In the bathroom, the first nurse helps Janie out of it, careful not to touch, and gives her a pair of sharp-creased hospital pajamas.

I want to see my brother are Janie's words to the woman.

Dinner was high speed and animal and without chat. Squash globbing knees, peas mortaring teeth, spoons clattering to the floor and snatched too late. Janie ached for sweet things and Ma said yes to pie, to ice cream, to fudge, take it.

Afterward, fog. A swaddling stupor. Someone passed gas, and Esther said, Touch-of-class Christmas. Look at us. Who here wants me to beat them at cards?

She was off to the living room speaking of big bands. Walt high-stepped to oversee the phonograph.

Ma also loved cards. What will we play for, she said, trailing.

Eddy said, In the spirit of the day, I say the loser must give the winner a gift.

Fair enough, said Pop. He favored card games of luck and had drunk past logic. In that case, I vote Crazy Eights.

Pop beat Esther. Janie sat beside her and watched her hold good twos and aces and fours and not play them.

When Pop knocked, Esther pouted, and when he laid down his last card, she threw hers down fast. She beat the sofa with her fist. She threw a throw pillow. Then sat up and said, Now. What will I give you?

When she put Janie's dress in his hands, she said, If it doesn't suit you, pass it on to someone you know.

Pop examined it without expression then yelled for Walt. Walter, he said. Get over here and play the hands-down winner of crazy eights.

Walt was digesting his seconds, losing the thread of it all. He beat Pop in no time and Pop grinned like a loser.

Whatever can a man like myself give a man like you? he said. Let the loser think on it, he added and took his drink outside.

They all played Casino for real then and forgot about Pop. When it was time to go, Ginny stuck her head outside, and there he was asleep by her tree with Walt's handsaw flung by in the snow. The teeth had bit the trunk in four wobbly places, none overlapping.

That's when Ma said to Eddy, Thanks.

The speaker is hungry and what lies on the other side Janie can no longer picture. She has not seen Donny in fourteen months. For a year he said her name and she made no answer. How to speak to what you cannot see? You invent it or else. Donny requires invention, so start with clothes. They are wearing the same pajamas. Supply them. Was Donny not balding? Subtract hair. Maybe he is this very minute reading a smut magazine. Janie offers up shower-capped bathing beauties. Though when she closes her eyes to summon this Donny, it is not Donny who answers the call but a woman. The woman is twenty, incurably hazardous, apart. Grown Janie does not look like Esther. She looks like no one and with terrible patience waits on Janie to speak. When Janie does, her tongue striking the roof of her mouth is loud. You can barely hear the words for the noise. Donny, are you there? I have something to tell you.

why did you leave?

3

HOW PEOPLE LIVE HERE

→→ *Belwick, 1978* ←←

AT ONLY FIVE O'CLOCK, DAD PUTS HIS HEAD IN THEIR DOOR AND says, You girls hungry? His head is hamburger round like Jean's own and full of math. Ruth's head is hot-dog skinny like Mom's. Ruth and Mom enjoy tragedy, those television movies where someone sweet dies calmly of tumors, or teenage boys taunt buffalo just minding their own business, bothering no one, or, the very worst, an American Indian girl is pushed inside a boiler room full of electricity out of sheer meanness. Just last weekend Mom and Ruth watched that one, tearing at big pancakes of caramel intended for apples. Then Mom popped a filling, then Monday she left.

The girls are not hungry but follow, with books. On the kitchen table are too many newspapers and toast crumbs, never good light to read by and never a sharp pencil to draw with. Jean will ask for an electric pencil sharpener for Christmas but will expect nothing. Last year she asked for a heavy-duty stapler. What she got was a poncho. Ruth and Jean push all the papers to one side and wait. Dad sets down a box of Triscuits. Next he brings a sweating cold stick of butter and a knife.

Dinner, he says. Dig in.

Jean asks if there is soup and Dad says not tonight.

He roots through the newspapers for Jobs and begins scanning with a pen that says BRIDGES FIBER OPTICS. The pens are defective—if you retract the tip it will not ever pop back—but there is two hundred count and no BRIDGES FIBER OPTICS left, so it is their duty, as Bridges, to use the pens, one by one, never retracting, until they are all used up.

Ruth eats no Triscuits. She keeps reading her library book, *Don't Hurt Laurie!* Laurie is, of course, despite the title, beaten with hairbrushes by her own mother and no doubt suffers from menses. Ruth cannot get enough of menses, menses and Nazis. Jean prefers books where things go uneventfully in well-thought-out houses. She cannot read a book without settling the floor plan, where the characters will pee and eat and sleep. Where their coats go. Some books are tricky and withhold. Just when she has assigned everyone a bedroom, got the dining room squared away, the central axis aligned to the sun's path so shadows tip nicely sideways, the story family goes haywire. In chapter six, they take hallways where none exist and step straight out of windows. They hang midair, sputtering, beseeching, *Miss Jean*—they are respectful and always a little Southern in their speech— *we're a goner. Save us, Miss Jean!* Then Jean has to put down the book and close her eyes. She has only six ready-made plans in her head. It is not enough. She cannot imagine what she has not seen, not reliably or well. She needs to get invited to more houses to play.

Jean eats two Triscuits with enough butter to make up for Ruth.

Dad says, You know, it's not forever. We'll tough it out.

We *know* that, says Ruth.

Mom left for summer school. Six weeks she will be gone. Every Saturday she will call. She is in Rutgers, New Jersey, getting a certificate to help drug addicts stop their lifestyle. Jean has never heard of Rutgers, but sees a city totally underground, totally wood paneled. She sees people with facial hair drinking sports beverages. Last spring, a real drug addict lived in their basement for a month, Tim. Tim was nineteen and very interested in muscles. Before that he was very interested in ephedrine, and before that methamphetamine. He had a mark on one cheek like a grape juice spill and no nail on his right pinkie. He used the bathroom stealthily, leaving no hairs. He did not eat with them. Mom carried down meatball subs and rotisserie chickens and gallons of sports beverages exclusive to Tim. Ruth told Jean, She gives him gifts. And when Tim was at the Y, helping people lift barbells, Ruth snuck down and Jean too. A punching bag hung from a new hook in the ceiling. It spun slowly, heftily, captive but dignified, like a gorilla in a zoo. *Try me*, it said, *I dare you*. The ceiling will fall in, said Ruth in her quiet factual voice, there's no way it can hold that thing. Taped to the wall behind the bag was a poster of a man with eyeliner, stretching his overlarge tongue to his chin. He looked like their neighbors' dog Gary after eating his own poop: disgusted but unrepentant. Beside that was a piece of Jean's best drawing paper with coiled boy print that said:

What if your Desires are not yours.

And Enslave Us.

What if They put them there.

What if that's how They do it.

What does that mean? Jean whispered.

He's mental, Ruth whispered, as if this, too, was fact and fulfilled her worst imaginings in the most satisfying possible way.

Dad slices a half-inch pat off the stick. He lays it between two Triscuits and inserts the whole thing in his mouth. This is a Dad thing, the installment of whole items in the mouth. It can be neither explained nor stopped. Jean has watched it happen to plums and small cupcakes, but the Triscuit business is new. She attends the swallow. Until grade three, Jean thought the Heimlich maneuver was a stern man in lederhosen who came and removed you in a headlock as penalty for careless chewing. Now she knows better but is not consoled.

Who wants to go for a ride? says Dad, preparing his next mouthful.

If you go out, says Ruth, can you get some food?

Like what? says Dad.

I don't care, says Ruth.

Give a hint, says Dad.

Fine, says Ruth, I don't care, I'll have a sub then. Ruth sighs. She can sigh entire paragraphs. Chicken parmigiana, she says, and a root beer, I guess.

Will that do it? says Dad. He has never fetched anything for anyone that Jean can recall.

Jean, who cannot even look at the cover of *Don't Hurt Laurie!*, has to sidle backward into their bedroom in case it is there, seeking eye contact from Ruth's bed, says, I'll come for a ride.

Both of you will come, says Dad.

Next door Gary starts up. The neighbors leave him outside with kibbles and go away for who knows how long, days, and the barking always starts like this, as simple communication. Someone is inside. Any moment they will open up. They just need to hear him. It takes an hour to shake this faith. Then Gary starts whining. Then howling. Then the yelps.

A dog is something they collude in wanting, Jean and Ruth, though Ruth wants it more. She wants it so ardently that Jean is a bit awed by the majesty of this longing. Jean wants a dog but she wants, also, with equal and indistinct longing, a dog bed and comb and ball, a dog's fondness for her. Nubby teats and whirl-pools of belly hair. Audible toenails. Can't we let Gary in? Ruth asks when Gary barks. Just while they're gone?

That dog is a nutcase, Dad says. They'd love that. You let that thing in, we'll never be rid of it.

Mom wants a dog, but not now. Any dog we get, she says, it will be on her to care for. Maybe later. After this summer, she says, we'll see.

When Tim left, he took their tape deck. It was not a good tape deck. It was half-busted, a spring broken somewhere so you had to rewind everything by hand with pencils. Dad never got to fix-ing it. That night late in their beds Jean lay faking sleep and Ruth lay reading and Dad's voice through the wall said, Was I right or what?

Mom answered low, It was a piece of crap, that's the last word.

I don't see the point, said Dad. Explain to me the point.

Talking to you is bad sex, said Mom. I'm done.

The girls get in the back of the Fiat together, and Dad says, What am I, a chauffeur? Jean moves to the front. Dad drives with just his knees, for pizzazz, and houses skid by almost exactly like their own. The flat part of Belwick was built by one guy with two ideas fifty years ago, Mom says. Ralph Matarossian designed two houses, flipped each once, and once again. Then he left for Lincoln. Since they moved here two years ago, Jean has visited enough of these houses to know where the bathroom is the moment the front door opens.

Dad does not think Belwick is so bad, if they could manage it. If he could get something going. He admires the ambition of the shrubs, how clean-edged they are, or sometimes spherical, and hopes the girls might appreciate how difficult, truly, this is to achieve with a clipper. This summer he tried to bonsai their boxwood. He was stunned how fast it got away from him. He kept removing to correct his mistakes until there was nothing, nothing left at all but a stub. The stub was so naked, he removed that too. Some things come back. Blueberries. He is not sure about boxwoods.

Will you look at that, he says and slows. In one lawn, three yews take the shape of a diamond, a heart, and a spade.

Jean looks. Wow, she says to be helpful. But the house, she can tell from the windows, is plan three, and no help to her at all.

This summer, Ruth has read in bed from morning until night, eating things with peanut butter, her hair fanned out on pillows. When you graduate grade four, haircuts are optional and Ruth has opted against. Her hair goes to her butt and the fanning takes time, and once accomplished, Ruth does not budge. She never wants to play. Not lava or bunnies, certainly not candynapper. Whenever Jean says, Want to play? Ruth says, Maybe later, we'll see, not looking up, and Jean sets out the bunnies for their talent show, just in case, rehearses them on their line kicks, coaches Huggypants on his sugarfoots, technically cheating, but Ruth keeps reading about menses and Nazis and girls beaten with hairbrushes, and when Jean says, Ready now? Ruth says, Maybe later.

Once, Jean left the bunnies on their marks for three days, just in case. Mom, sick of the mess, the house, *relentless Belwick*, saying *how do people live here*, put the bunnies in a trash bag and the bag on the street. But when the trash truck took the bag, she flagged it three blocks down to retrieve it. Jean hates to see their parents defeated in parenting. She accepted the bunnies' reappearance without comment, as if they had never left.

The sub shop is in the Center. Dad double-parks while Ruth runs in.
Did you want something? Dad asks Jean.
Jean does and does not. She wants to take no sides. She chews her thumb. Maybe a drink, she says.
Have you ever had a Shirley Temple? Dad asks. That I bet you'd like. He chuckles.
Jean says what's a Shirley Temple, and Dad says when Ruth gets her sandwich, they will go for a spin and try one—how would she like that? Jean senses something wrong with the plan, nothing she can name. She wants to say *are we allowed*, but that would be the worst thing.

This summer, Jean's brain has forgotten the how-to of sleep. Not every night, but sometimes. The silence takes some getting used to. Jean listens to her heart beating and she listens to herself swallow and to Ruth snore and when it rains it is deafening. Sometimes, possessed by monstrous bravery, Jean gets up and walks the house. The furniture in the half-made morning looks half-made: small and violet, implausible. It looks like Fimo. She stands in the thresholds, her breath loud. She imagines herself a stranger snuck in from the street and thinks, *I wonder who lives here*. She peers at the bodies of her parents under sheets, limp and hot, watches their big nostrils quiver, feels the make-believe strangeness as truth and wonders if she will remember any of this in the day. She will not, she thinks, and perhaps because of this, does not.

Now they are driving uphill. The houses are bigger. The sun is a fireball burning up the tree line, throwing shadows down to meet them. Belwick Hill came after Belwick. When Ralph Matarossian dug out the basements for the houses on the flats, he piled all the dirt on the edge of town and called the heap the Hill. Each house here is different from the last and secretive about it. Each stands back from the road behind conspiring shrubs, also secretive, not gabbing with passersby about playing cards but standing tall and wild as trees. The house parts visible are almost castles. Jean wishes she could get in a turret, for research. If she could scout sites, she could read more.

Ruth knows the right way to get places. Why are we going this way? she says. This is the opposite of home.

On the back side of the Hill, the sun is so fierce they all three shield their eyes with their arms, in synch like choreography. Jean likes that. She wishes that happened more often, ideally by chance, if not, then by rehearsal. In television, yes, people cooperate in random acts of tap dance without forethought or coercion and it excites Jean. In life, almost never. When the Hill bottoms out and the Bridges remove their arms, Belwick is done. A sign speaks mildly of Watertown. Dad pulls beside a medical supply shop where the mannequins are happy amputees, grinning in paper gowns. In the window, one balances a bedpan on wrist stumps. Another wields a walker with elbows. Beside this shop is a place, all brick, no windows, with a sign that reads SHEA'S. The walk in front looks sticky.

Dad parallel parks and nails it. He is good at driving.

We can't go in there, says Ruth.

Dad says it's all right. He explains about the Shirley Temples.

Ruth says she will wait in the car.

Suit yourself, says Dad. We won't be long. Ready, Jean?

Jean hesitates. She hates to see her parents defeated, but what is there behind that brick? She does not know. She is afraid to know.

You don't want to come, says Dad, fine.

Jesus, Ray, says Aunt Eugenia. A sleepover! To Jean and Ruth she says, Doesn't give a person much notice, does he? Kind of springs up on a person, doesn't he, girls?

Dad says be good. He will be back in the morning.

In the living room where they have been only for Thanksgiving, every surface bears witness to the undeniable facts of puff art: buy five copies of the same drugstore card, cut out the pictures, layer them with Elmer's. 3D out of 2D—that is how. Aunt Eugenia explains it every year. Ruth sits on the sofa with the sub bag on her lap and her book open. Aunt Eugenia says, Jean, doll, let me do your hair up nice. Come close by the mirror. I won't bite, doll, mother of God. There, good girl. Your dad's lucky, all girls. It could have been worse. Me with all boys, will you believe it? They won't let me touch them. Will you believe that? Look at you two, identical eyebrows, I could eat you up, she says, but is wrong. Jean's and Ruth's eyebrows are notably unalike. Jean's are lopsided like Dad's, the left surprised by what the right has failed to see. Mom and Ruth have frowny brows that fan toward the temple.

Aunt Eugenia piles all Jean's hair on Jean's head in a mess and considers this, as if Jean's head is for sale.

My hair, says Aunt Eugenia, stacking her own head above Jean's in the mirror, is finally almost exactly what I want, and I can't tell you the time it's taken or the money I've spent. You'd die.

She pulls Jean's hair down and back and twists it tight at the base of Jean's skull.

What defeats a person, Aunt Eugenia says, is the nose. The nose has a mind of its own. And I can tell you the nose you see here is not the nose I started off with. Oh no, doll. I had a nose like a little radish, would you believe it?

You can choose your friends, not your family, isn't that right, girls? Aunt Eugenia says when they are quiet.

Your mom will be back, says Aunt Eugenia. For God's sake, don't look so grim.

We *know* that, says Ruth from the sofa.

And I'll tell you something else, Aunt Eugenia says, the good thing about Bridges men is that they change the oil and they calculate the tip. You think you need chitchat? You don't. I know I don't look it, but I'm older than your mom, and trust me, you're happy for the quiet. Your mom was a wild thing, blood can't be helped, but people settle. That they do.

Jean, doll, don't cry, says Aunt Eugenia.

She's not crying, says Ruth.

Well, she is, says Eugenia, and can you blame her?

Which is better, honest or nice? Jean asked her teacher on the last day of third grade. It was urgent that she know that minute, though the next day she would not remember why or care—it was as if a different kid asked it on a different planet, that is how those questions are—and Mr. Mulford fingered his comb-over like someone manually straightening his thoughts. Art, he said finally. Art is best.

Jean poked Dad that night and asked what that meant. Dad was watching a show about Komodo dragons mating, but perhaps did not know it. His eyes were mostly closed. On the floor by his chair were the open mouths of bottles, exhaling beer breath. Jean repeated the question, and Dad said, Mr. Mulford who?

He seemed earnest in his unfamiliarity with the name Mr. Mulford.

We have a play date, Ruth tells Eugenia. At seven.

You do? Well, gosh. I wish your father had said something, because your cousin Jim has the car.

Ruth says it is walking distance, a block away on the Hill. She says she just needs to check the number.

Ruth hunts through Aunt Eugenia's phone book. Jean asks for what, and Ruth says hush.

The only people they know near Aunt Eugenia, at the Hill's foot but higher, are the Sterns. Miri and Lisi are the same grades as Ruth and Jean. They are classmates, not friends. Ruth, who never forgets where anything is, knows the outside of their house from sleepaway carpool. She calls on the kitchen phone and what she says, away from Eugenia, is this: We were wondering if you want us to come over and play.

When Mom left for Rutgers, she packed the backseat of the Nissan to the very top with all her favorite clothes. When she backed out she tore off three peonies but did not stop. Gary chased her to School Street, then drifted sideways tracking pigeon. On a bush, pinned up debonairly by wind, was a Kleenex, which he ate.

The Stern hedge is dense. You could stow things in it and Ruth does. She stows her sub bag and her book.

Miri and Lisi answer the front door in slippers the size of toasters. The slippers are furry and orange, with horse pinheads and yarn manes and skinny limbs splayed uselessly sideways. Shoes off, says Miri, that's a house rule. Jean and Ruth hand over their sandals to their hosts, who take them and disappear. Jean and

Ruth wait in the foyer. The house is unlike any Jean has seen, she can sense it, is primed already for plan number seven.

What do you play? Miri calls from somewhere unseen. We're supposed to be playing.

Jean and Ruth trace the voice to a room as tall as their school gym, full of yellow couches dissected into one-person pods and walls covered every inch in books. In a fireplace hang two Santa feet, although it is July. Beside the fireplace is a glass door.

Miri looks at Jean looking at the feet. So what? she says, we're Jewish. Half-Unitarian. *You* look like you're itching to make stuff with cotton balls. What do you two play?

Sometimes we play . . . Jean looks at Ruth for help, but Ruth is studying a set of photos on the wall. They are framed black-and-white shots of a pretty woman with big pupils, sitting uncomfortably in a tree, Miri and Lisi barking up from the base like dogs at a squirrel. Left to right, each photo shows the woman higher in the tree, the girls below more frenzied, in some shots levitating.

Sometimes we read books, offers Jean. Sometimes we play music, but our mother gave our tape player to a drug addict she's helping. It's her career.

Miri is lying back in her own personal pod, folding and unfolding her spindly legs up to her chin.

Our mother edits the nation's preeminent medical journal. Miri speaks with closed eyes. She goes by Dr. Fairbottom.

Mother would like to add the two of us together and divide us in half, says Lisi. Miri's sensuous and linguistic. I'm nervous and computational.

Miri brings both knees to her chin and clasps them with two arms like a compacted umbrella, then squints at Jean so long without blinking that Jean wonders if it is a game for which she does not know the rules. Then Miri plucks a loose thread from the tweedy pod cushion and addresses it.

Jean does crafts, Miri informs the thread, with Popsicle sticks.

Tell them about the sky, says Lisi. Tell them why it's not really blue.

Miri wedges the thread between her teeth and lets it dangle, her eyes half-lidded.

Guess how many times Miri can pogo without stopping, says Lisi. She tries a pirouette. She skids in her slippers, then sitting hard on the wood floor, works an ankle behind her neck. It will not quite go.

Last week, Miri auditioned for the TV show *MacGyver*, says Lisi from the floor. Actresses make the same as heart surgeons. It's true.

Miri looks not at Lisi or Ruth but at Jean.

What's wrong with your face? she says to Jean.

Jean thinks of the three people in life she has hated for more than a day—Michael Driscoll, Ginny Sinkel, and Peter Price—and decides she will hate Miri Stern longer. She wants to run through every room in the house, then leave. Through the glass door she sees what looks like an office. A curly head shifts above a leather headrest. The chair does not move or turn.

We don't play anything, says Ruth. We watch TV. All day long we watch *MacGyver*.

Miri looks at Ruth like something old she has found an unexpected use for.

Lisi says, We don't even *own* a TV.

We'll play in the basement, says Miri, standing up. I know you—she eyes Jean—are itching for a grand tour of the house, but this furniture is brand-new, and as you can see, completely white.

Jean surveys the yellow couches and says nothing. Her stomach growls.

Miri shepherds Jean and Ruth ahead, Lisi trailing, hopping on one foot. Jean passes a dining room, a kitchen, a room with three treadmills. She tries not to appear interested.

Miri stops them by a door that opens to pitch black. Use the switch, says Miri, or walk in darkness, your choice.

Jean finds a set of switches and flips until the lights come on.

Not *that* one. Miri points to the red switch Jean has flipped.

Lisi arranges her face in an expression of horror, covers it with her hands, and sobs. Her shoulders heave.

That one calls the fire department, says Miri. It costs six hundred dollars to send men. When they get here they're going to be hopping mad. They'll throw a fit. They have to be paid immediately or they start breaking things with pickaxes.

Ruth grabs Jean's arm and pulls.

She pulls Jean down the hall toward the foyer.

Stay out of Mother's office! calls Miri.

They backtrack. They cannot find their sandals. Ruth finds the front door, pulls Jean out, leaves the door ajar, pounds barefoot to the street. Behind them, Lisi can be heard faintly screaming, Pogo state champ second runner-up!

They don't turn.

Ruth stops only to extract her sub and book from the hedge, then breaks into a run.

Together Ruth and Jean run. They zigzag through strange lawns. Their feet feel good, the grass slick. Only graveled driveways slow them. They move in synch without plan or negotiation.

What's wrong with *your* face! yells Ruth.

We don't even *own* a TV! yells Jean, laughing, running harder, and the streets produce houses, each unlike the last, whose bright insides she can see and steal and no one anywhere can stop her.

It will take a long time to get home on foot. But Ruth has a plan. They will hitchhike. No one hitchhikes in Belwick; that's why it's safe. When they reach home, Jean will squeeze through the bathroom window and unlock the door for Ruth, and Ruth will call the Rutgers number for Mom, although it is not Saturday, and if Tim answers, or any man, they will let Gary in and feed him chicken parmigiana and show him kindnesses of every sort and even when the neighbors return, even when Dad comes back, at dawn, with the rooms violet and a cut on his forehead and two policemen, it will be too late: Gary will already be their dog.

how did you meet?

4

DICKY LUCY

Cambridge, 1967

I WAS A GREEN-EYED, BEE-HIVED GORILLA. I WAS THE WILD GIRL
of Brighton. Nobody knew. I had a nineteen-inch waist and a D
cup; they called me the Shelf; I cannot account for you girls. After
your Gramp broke my nose and my arm, I moved. I lived at the Y.
By day I kept up at Girls' Latin. I kept up my grades, the scholar-
ship, nobody knew. We had uniforms, white and navy. Kneesocks
and ascot. I kept mine pressed and clean because I loved them.
When I met your father, it was easy not to tell him things. He
never told me things, too. About money he in effect lied. It takes
one to know one, but that applied to me, not him. The year was
'67. Men like that never saw themselves as prey.

When I met him, did I think *house?* Did I think *bedsheets, yard,
breakfast nook?* Did I think *patio?* That, and *dog* and *guinea pig*
and *cat* and *hamster* and *turtle* and *dwarf rabbit* and, with some
luck, *horse.* I wanted animals. I wanted a brass knocker and a sing-
ing doorbell, the melody "Que Sera." A wreath of baby gourds
for Thanksgiving, gooseberries for Christmas. There would be
a mantel and on it seasonal elves. The Easter baskets would be

excessive. I'd litter the house with fat foil eggs, each one oozing a gold sugar yolk. Underfoot for months they'd be. I did, yes, think so, very much. I thought ballet lessons like everyone else thought but also roller skating lessons and ice skating lessons and painting lessons, and a Formica bar in the basement where a person could paint—I don't know why I thought you paint at a bar—and naturally, then, my thoughts needed you.

You ask about your father. That is half what I thought when we met.

When we met I nursed Dicky Lucy. At nineteen Dicky Lucy rolled a Chevy going eighty. The break was C1, the highest vertebra. When his mother, Mrs. Lucy, hired me on, I didn't know I was the fifth. I was volunteering with quad vets then, answering phones at Doody Diapers. I wanted weekend work. I'm not a nurse, I said on the phone, I got through one term but then what happened—

Do you chatter? Mrs. Lucy said. His best topic is boxing. Dicky hates world affairs, and when you come wear three-inch heels if you're under five five, a Cross Your Heart brassiere if you've got it, and stockings with seams. Show your figure, but not tarty. Are you any good with a gun?

I fed Dicky Lucy deviled ham on white rolls and floretted his pickles. I maneuvered his straw. I got him from his chair to the tub with the aid of a board. I scrubbed him and shaved him with sting-free kiddie soap. He had such a lot of hair. He was like my father in that. I combed his duckbill with a greasy grab of Vaseline and held a hand mirror to him, combed it four, ten times, until he was well pleased. We played Chinese checkers. I moved his marbles, illegal moves at his word and his voice that drill. My job was to lose and bemoan the loss. My job was to cut pictures from magazines and paste them in an album with rubber cement and no wrinkles at all:

muscle cars and Ursula Andress. If the picture bubbled anywhere, Dicky Lucy said burn it. My job was to shoot Dicky Lucy's pump gun out the window at squirrels in the oaks. How humanly they shrieked. How the cantilevered limbs groaned with their running and sometimes fell. I missed and I missed. What else could I do? Dicky Lucy's *get him*s and my aim so poor. My sympathy lay with anything furred.

Dicky Lucy stayed midweek at a hospital in Weymouth, but on weekends he got dropped at his mother's. She lived back-to-back to Idy Bridges. Their porches faced off across a shared plot of knotweed that Idy was hard-set and ill-equipped to kill. Ray, Idy's youngest, was the last at home, work-study at Northeastern. He had a cherry Ford he tinkered with, Dicky Lucy knew well. At four every Sunday, Dicky Lucy made me dial. I hated telephones then the way I now hate cameras. A liar piece, my voice coming at you and pitched all wrong. Like with a gun, I could never seem to aim straight. Even my breathing on the phone to me sounds like a lie.

Why, hello, Ray, I'd say. It's Jane, at Dicky's. We were just wondering if you happened to be heading out, if it was not too much out of your way—

Weymouth was on the way to nowhere and Dicky Lucy was a hardship.

Dicky Lucy was vain.

And always, yes, your father would come.

Studious Ray; student of how objects transfused power, one to the other, a particulate sharing, like the transfusions, one to the other, blood or germ, of the living.

(Ray would correct me on this. Electrical engineering isn't like that, he'd say.)

And the way Ray hefted Dicky Lucy from his chair at the door to his Ford at the curb, the way Dicky Lucy needled him—

someday, I'll let you work on my toaster, smart guy—that worked on me too.

It was the other half of my thinking.

It began the way things begin for men, with cars.

Before cars it would have had to have been horses. Before that, what? What else can men own and strap on and make be fast?

They were neighbors, Dicky Lucy and Ray, and they had gone to grade school and high school together but were not friends. Dicky Lucy was two grades ahead. This was when Rindge and Latin was two schools. Latin trained kids for college. Rindge trained kids for typing and plumbing, woodwork and metalwork and engines and babies. Ray had won some fame in his grade school days as the local whiz kid TV repairman, but it was Dicky Lucy, not Ray, who went on to Rindge. Mrs. Lucy gossiped with the indiscretion of the long-term lonely.

Sundays Ray would say just *I'll be over.*

He was, and took Dicky, and I'd take the train home.

But that day, for no reason, he said my name. And how it feels to hear a person say your name is only one of two things—happy or sick. The body keeps its decisions streamlined like that.

He said, Jane. You feel like taking a ride?

Then as now a man of small economies.

I packed Dicky Lucy's Weymouth bag. Within a quarter hour out front the Ford idled. The engine cut out. The door slammed but after too many seconds, into which I read *qualm* or *duty* or possibly *cigarette*. I put down the paste pot. The cement fumes got to me, and Ursula, like every trapped thing in there, began to look complicit and paid. She looked professionally malevolent, like she was driving a sled. I held the album page out to Dicky to vet. Not like that, he said, closer. In the light, he said, here. Goddamn, Jane. Turn it this way.

But my technique was good. He seemed disappointed.

I listened for footsteps. Mrs. Lucy waved me over to her iron-ing board, where she chain-played three staggered hands of Patience and offered me ten dollars plus mail-in coupon to dye my hair blonde. I told her I wouldn't. She pulled the coupon from the socket of her breasts. It was pressed to a pill.

I detoured Dicky Lucy for the window, paused by The Castle (a picture someone had painted on glass in reverse, a feat of per-versity that Mrs. Lucy and I took time to puzzle at: they must have painted it outside in, highlights then outer stone then inner stone then black, and when I looked at the painting I heard the turning of a key), then made a stop at Robin Redbreast (from the nuns' same yard sale, sequins on cotton ticking—*hand sewn by girls of twelve in the Philippines!* Mrs. Lucy said, aghast and gratified by the human cost of art, and the key fell away to the bottom of a well), and I tried to look like someone wanting air, not escape. I listened for footsteps in the same way the Lucys listened for mine, I imagine. That apartment was tightly crammed with Lucys. They were just two in five rooms, but they expanded to fill them. The place overheated. It smelled of pet store. Mice by the pound and interbreeding, although Dicky Lucy kept no pet.

Mrs. Lucy, said Ray—not, *how've you been, Dick.*

What I noticed usually when Ray entered was the disquieting size of his head. It was big. Blockish. Cowlicks feathered it. Yet that day there was something nicely transparent to the structure of it all: Cro-Magnon brows making caves for eyes, which were also big and set on the outer reaches of the face, like eyes of the hunted, optimized to see what's coming, field of view not depth, retiring and appraising but not afraid. They recalled to me the eyes of goats. Below those were the cliff-drop cheeks. Caliper legs. The neat and outsized hands of the handy. Ray looked like he would be good with a bow and arrow. My people earned as lookalikes and gamblers, and by habit I asked myself, *Who does he look like?* The answer you know from the movies I fed you—Tony Curtis minus the dandy, plus Steve McQueen's straight shooting minus the smartass—is less right than the answer you can't know, Eddy.

I could smell it on him. *Smoke* not *duty*.

Mrs. Lucy (*Queen for a Day* fan and aspirant) said, Ray, before you and Dicky head out, be a doll and fix the set? The picture isn't right. I keep getting fuzz.

Mrs. Lucy spoke always of heading *out*, not *back*: like they were two pals, rogues, out to paint the town red. In Ray's pocket she tucked an envelope she thought I didn't see.

While Ray folded himself down to the RCA, Mrs. Lucy told the legend of TV Ray. How when Ray was four, the Bridges were the first on the block to get a television set. Ray's father was a natural fixer. He had been promoted from subway driver to subway inspector and wore a badge like a policeman that he let Ray hold. When the TV broke, the repairman was stealthy. Trade secrets—he didn't want Ray's father to watch him working. So Ray's father and brothers left the room and Ray stayed, the youngest, playing one-man conkers with chestnuts on the floor. When the work was done and paid for, Ray's father showed that repairman out. Ray, his father said to him then, What have we got? Ray pocketed his winning chestnut (a two-er). Then he asked for a Phillips head screwdriver, removed the TV's backing, and indicated the new capacitor.

(Mrs. Lucy didn't say it then but later how that same week was when Ray's father died. One morning he was inspecting subways. The next he said to Idy, his wife and alarm clock, give me five minutes. He pulled the covers over his head and never woke.)

Ray, like his father, liked to fix things. You enjoyed watching him work the way you enjoyed watching him spoon up chowder.

You begged tastes from his bowl, though you hated clams. If I fixed you your own, you wouldn't touch it.

Ray tried to show you about fixing. That it takes not talent but willingness to break what you hoped to fix. He knew defeat as disinterested, a condition of life and not of people. You hated to hear it. The way some stake all on the existence of the divine, you staked all on the existence of talent, and found, in its absence as in its presence, proof. Ray has less interest in failure than anyone I know. I think failure must be the bad hobby of narcissists, as the devil is the bad hobby of the devout.

What I'm saying is that your father was no baby. Ray had this easy rectitude he didn't know about. Mine was a forgery. Not to say fake. But those of us who must forge it admire that not knowing.

This all made Ray maddening to would-be bullies. I could see that.

And I could see it in Ray's back how he hated this story of Mrs. Lucy's. What he would not say lodged low on his spine. Where quite suddenly I wanted to touch.

Dicky Lucy watched me watch Ray at the TV and snapped his gum. His tongue was strong; he liked to body build what he could. He enjoyed toothpicks. He opened wide for me to lay them in. He spat them out in his can. He was always working something around in his mouth.

Goddamn, Ma, he said. We don't have time to goose around. TV Ray, what say we split?

Ray fiddled the tuner and rose. That should do it, he said to Mrs. Lucy. (*After* and not *before* it was true. The allergy to exaggeration. I say in twenty years you never took me to a movie. Well, Ray says. I thought we saw three.)

Jane will join us, Ray informed The Castle.

Dicky spat in his can. He flashed big gums. A date for TV Ray, he said as if to himself. He looked for me, but I was not there. I was halfway down the stairs with the bag.

Sure she will, I heard him say.

I always left before Ray lifted Dicky. When I lifted him for baths, we played the match on the radio. It was important to have near us the loud and comfortable sounds of regulated hitting. Dicky couldn't even compose an arm. They were arms once given to showboating (the first day Mrs. Lucy put me in a chair with a shoebox of photos, smiling pimpishly or maternally or both, and did not budge until I'd thumbed through all, and I learned that mobile Dicky had been stocky, procamera, pro-Elvis, pro-prom, and a wrestler, never without well-placed sidekicks; that Dicky Lucy favored the stranglehold). Now those sleeves waggled, light nearly as sleeves.

I know nothing about cars. Sometimes I walk to the wrong one and wonder for a minute why my key won't work. I suppose Ray's was beautiful. It shined in that street in a way that seemed to please him. As he brought Dicky Lucy out, he kept his eyes down as if in modesty. Maybe he had just washed it. I don't know how to desire a car. What nonpeople earn that check box, beauty? For men like Ray and Dicky Lucy, it's what they can put their hands on and ride: cars, horses, girls, boats, and motorbikes. They would never speak of beauty in a table or a fish or another man's baby. For women it's what they can put in a room, and their body is another kind of room. We learn to desire pearls, not oysters. Husbands, not men. We learn to want what we can affix to ourselves. For men, we practice a weird rehearsal, desiring ourselves as if we were men in order to learn how to be desired.

Dicky said, You kids take front.

We already had.

Ray took Mass. Ave to Fresh Pond Parkway to 2. I had been passenger on this route in all brands of jalopies, with all brands of unfitness to operate vehicles. It was a losing experience that had made me duller, not sharper. In car passenger seats I had to right the urge to be luggage. My job as Dicky's nurse and Ray's date was to be a person. I hoped to find a hawk so I could point it out *Look.*

Dicky Lucy said: The radio's broke?

The window's broke?

Your foot broke?

Ray found a station Dicky did not fault. He took the Ford to seventy. The hood hiccupped and the dashboard too.

Don't stay mad, Ace, said Dicky Lucy.

Dicky Lucy said: Ace, tell us a story. We had us some good times in high school, tell her. TV Ray, my only friend. God we were tight. You don't love me no more like you used to, Ace. At night I cry. Tell her how you used to hang around the woodshop hoping to see me. Dicky, you used to say, Dicky, teach me how to live, teach me what it means to—

Knock it off, said Ray.

Dicky Lucy went quiet back there. The Ford jittered on to some dated music. I dated it to their high school years—maybe. I could only pretend to know, as I could only pretend to musical taste. It took me time to figure it out: music is what you find in high school, and where you find it is, my hunch, at friends' houses. My high school years lacked a house, so they lacked friends' houses, since you did not accept what you couldn't return. So they lacked music. How little I knew had a way of offending people.

Ray would pick it up, Dicky Lucy said louder than necessary, but we're flat maxed out. Fifth gear's shot to hell, a real pisser.

Dicky shouted: We'd like to open her up, Jane, but we can't do it. Cannot. Want to and can't. The clutch is a bitch.

There's nothing wrong with it, said Ray, and pushed it to ninety.

Dicky said: Easy, Ace. You'll muss my hair.

We now had the left lane all to ourselves. The car had assumed a syncopated rolling motion that seemed not exactly bad and at least rhythmic. It rolled along to Chuck Berry, and I tried to think of something I heard someone say about Berry to repeat. Berry is the best, I imagined myself saying, but I'd have had to shout it and possibly defend it. I looked for any bird of prey at all.

Did I mention that being driven in cars, when car or driver is off, makes me want to disappear? To be a glove of myself? To stow away in the glove compartment? Every bit of blood in me gunned for my feet, slammed there, flip-turned, gunned for my heart. It's a terrible thing to feel your blood doing laps inside you. If they could induce it, they would torture with it. They'd make nonbelievers pray. I found myself praying to Franny, *help*.

Dicky said: Having fun yet, Jane?

Ray held steady to Yankee Division Highway when up from the floor came the thick and dire smell of burnt hair. Ray sat up straight. He set the Ford south. My silence seemed a bad agent, a bad hand on the wheel. Berry was out on parole, I thought to say, or was it the other, and then Berry was gone and it was Cline strung out wailing "So Wrong" and I had nothing on Patsy Cline.

Dicky said, Let's vote. Can we? Who thinks this date's a pisser? Can we speak our hearts? At this juncture, I feel that I can. I say this date's a pisser and I say you're not speaking your hearts and I love you kids like I love myself. That's what hurts. Ray, let's turn it around. Let's go the long way, show Janie a good time.

Yankee Division was the newish beltway, the first of its kind. It had a residual hick feel then. For stretches there was nothing but state-owned trees. The road's shoulder banked sharply down to softwoods.

The car floor palpitated. In relief I saw it down there near me. Mrs. Lucy's envelope.

Is that yours? I could say to Ray at last.

As I reached for it Ray said leave it but I said I had it and Ray took a hand off the wheel to beat me to it and Dicky crooned, *I've seen the light, darlin', I'll make it right.*

The car pulled right, jumped the shoulder, and nose-dived the bank. Each rut in the bank telegraphed itself to our spines as pine needles rushed to enfold us. Dicky's voice vibratoed. The last thing I heard was a high-pitched hooting from the rear, a sound I could not place until later at Mass General as Dicky Lucy's laughter.

We all survived this, no one unchanged.

The dashboard snapped two of my ribs, my collarbone, and rebroke my broken nose.

Dicky regained sensation in his feet. A medical anomaly, unwelcome both to the doctors, who could not explain it, and to Dicky, who could not scratch the toes that itched him.

Ray, protected in the enclave of the floor space, came out of it intact, all eight points of his cranium accounted for, but carless and amorous. I was in rehab two weeks. On each day he visited, Ray sat sweating on a green shell chair at my bedside in the same navy suit and navy-striped tie, elbows propped on knees. He suffered to converse with me. He brought me maple candies molded in the shape of maple leaves. Somehow, in his romantic detective work, he had hit upon the bad information that I loved seahorses, and each day brought me a different seahorse token—statuettes, jewelry boxes, pendants, pins. I had been much in hospitals throughout my childhood, and his solicitude, and his mistake, touched me with its excess. It was a brand of excess I craved. I asked him to remove that suit. I asked him to roll up his sleeves and side part his hair like Eddy. We weren't much for talk and shared a distaste for ceremony. The day I left Mass General, I conceived Ruth. The Brighton courthouse was our second date.

When Mrs. Lucy advised a week after my discharge that I find a husband, since care for Dicky in my fragile state was impractical, I was not quite truthful. I said that I would try.

are you real?

5

HOW I MISS YOU

→→ *Boston, 1987* ←←

HARVARD SQUARE

Twenty-five kids board the car. All but four decline to sit. The decision happens without talk and is instantly irreversible. They will stand until Park Street, fixed to rails in subtly polarized teenagery compounds.

They are on a field trip to the city, maybe wishing this less obvious. Mr. Mulford herding. Their mission is photographs, to take and to see. The ICA has a show of the guy who breaks wall-high faces into swatches.

The bus part was old, but the T is a win. Belwick High School promotes a belwickiocentric model of the universe, and the subway confounds this cosmology in a way that relieves the kids, unknots their necks where the camera straps bite, makes them want to become farmers, or artists, or at the very least diarists. The subway confounds with brown people, bandaged people, warty people, punks, and the frank, arousing stench of pee.

This end of the Red Line is not much less white. But the bandaged. There a taped nose, there a wrapped knee. Not casts but those splogey foot splints you know cover fester. It is as though everyone en masse had something malign and secret removed. The festerers might be subjects, if the kids had the nerve to ask. You cannot shoot without asking. Of course, commuters in jewel tones read about love and vampires, but they are incidental. They have had nothing removed. They are not part of the experience and do not warrant photography.

Sitting together are the Mulford pets. Four strong, united in sexlessness.

With Jean, it is genes. At twelve her body hit pause. Hers is a smallness just shy of freakdom, still proportionate, laughable. It disarms the world. It makes the world smile to itself. Girls her age coo in her face. Classmates pick her up in the hall. They see her size as a personality trait and her as a toy. She sees it as a rate problem: other people grow too fast. She does not want to make the world smile. On the contrary.

With Smurf and Ugly, mothers are implicated. One meaty and schizo, hoarding trash, talking all the time of poop to Smurf. The other frail and super-Mormon, counting Ugly's calories.

With Lusik—well, Lusik is foreign. Getting foreigner by the day out of spite, if Belwick would only notice. In the two years since she moved here from the place no one cares about—*Muslim? Hindu? Zionist? Yes*, she says, *dumb-ass, I'm Zionist*—her accent has thickened.

Your English is so good. Where are you from?

Thanks, and you? Where are you from? Your English is mediocre.

How she misses Mossi. If there is a word for it, it has slipped the crack between Armenian and English.

The brakes give a womanish scream. All twenty-five ignore it.

Peter Hunig, hair quite pubic, asks Lusik if her haircut is self-inflicted. Mossi's last do for her. You should shave it, Mossi said. Not yet, she said, no. Give me a Bettie Page but short on one side.

The pets run the journal. They published Peter's leprosy limerick, but is he grateful?

I love my hair, Lusik informs Peter without looking up. She is writing to Mossi in London. Trying to stick to Armenian, but she uses it now only to fight with their father or cook with their mother, and the letter comes out like a squalling baby. *Baba's an ass about you. He can disown me too. What does he know? He never even met Michael, not that I have, but I'm sure he's everything you say. I'll buy my own ticket for June. I'll help you and Michael with rent, work in a lab, do summer school there, get done with this dogshit for good in ten weeks—*

Ugly and Smurf practice their madrigal duet, not embarrassed to sing.

Smurf is wearing gloves for hygiene. Ugly is in her overalls. Still, with her high-gloss hair and advanced ski-slope nose, she looks like a silkscreen empress. Her smile is a kind of safe sex, dispensed free to the viewer.

Your voice gives me chills, says Peter to Smurf. How much for you to lick that handrail? I'll give you twenty bucks.

Look who it is, says Smurf to Ugly. Someone Special.

Jean deploys aggressive empathy stylings. Peter, how *are* you. I was just thinking of you and I have three questions.

What's your problem, Peter? says Julie Bosko. Why can't you leave us alone? She is hanging off the rail above the pets, way too close.

Jean knows the pets agree:

There is something low-grade yet annoying about Julie Bosko, and it is not just her allergy to pine nuts, which she invokes on all occasions, even when a person is just ordering pizza, pizza that in no way involves Julie.

Pizza that asks nothing of Julie.

Sweat gives her hives.

Also latex.

It is that Julie Bosko sees the world as a conspiracy of pine nuts and sweat and latex, when in fact the world was just doing its laundry, taking no notice of her.

There is also the problem of her breasts. They are spry and individuated, large, and not entirely of one mind with Julie. Julie Bosko is dull, but the breasts are edgy and not without ambition. Go-getters.

KENDALL/MIT

College people swarm the rails. Ectomorphs, safe shoes. Brains stewing in science.

What troubles Jean is ionization. She pulls out her sketchbook and tries drawing what happens to sodium. She can't draw it. Cannot grasp it. Cannot grasp degrees and kinds of bonds, when, in the world apparent, there is only one bond, absolute.

If it were not for Lusik, Jean would never ace chemistry. If it were not for Jean, Ugly would not ace physics. If it were not for Ugly, Smurf would not pass biology.

There is nothing Lusik would not ace if it were not for them.

Lusik gets degenerate orbitals and noble gas cores, Dada, Stein, and the No Problem Orchestra. She can pronounce without effort all French vowels.

Though the three will have choices, they will go wherever Smurf's GPA can take her. Jean can see this as if it has already happened. It is as necessary and right as the receiving ground when you fall. Ugly's parents and Lusik's will have to face the music. The music of pet fidelity! Jean's will not hear any music. College? they will say. Well, good for you. Her sister, Ruth, spent senior year in the attic, no one the wiser till June.

But lately, whenever Jean calls Lusik for chemistry help, Lusik's mother answers. Dozens of calls, yet she never seems to know Jean. Each time, Jean identifies herself, and Lusik's mother says *oh* in a disheartened way and waits. Keeps waiting. Keeps waiting. Like time and will might undo the fact of Jean. Finally and without warning, the mom calls up to Lusik in her own language, a stream of imposing length and force whose meaning Jean cannot know but whose sound slurry she has memorized. When Lusik comes on, Jean always asks, What did she say? But Lusik just laughs that laugh.

Jean gives up on sodium and draws these scientist hairlines. It is hairlines, more than noses or chins, that make a person look himself. For a while Jean thought she could be the cop artist who draws how victims recall their attackers. Then she read that the victim's memory is half the time wrong.

What they have together, the pets, is this great thing, a heavy thing, carry it and it feeds even as it depletes you. It is like a tick but good, a tick that keeps you company and of which you cannot be free.

CHARLES STREET/MGH

The train pulls aboveground, onto the Longfellow Bridge. There are no signs urging you to call the Samaritans. They are busy people and it is not that high.

On with the scrubs. Off with the warty. Below the river presses on, indifferent.

Certain things are barred. No homeless person sleeping shots. No Hi Mom shots. No posed hilarity shots. No going AWOL in the Combat Zone. These are ways to fail. Between Park Street and the ICA, they will stop over in the Garden. There for an hour they can be individuals on the loose expressing themselves, finding stuff to shoot. The pets plan to be individuals expressing themselves in a clump while eating fried dough.

It's hard to fail art, I won't kid you, Mr. Mulford says. His voice is loud. The art room is his natural habitat. Outside it some quality of Mulfordness is lost. He goes three-dimensional and strange. You see his skull more. Mr. Mulford frowns. C, all right, *C-* for Julie and her passion for fashion sketches, which we *hate*.

Julie Bosko smiles. You want to be called out.

But to *fail* takes great cunning or great stupidity, and a delicious Hoodsie to any of you who succeed by either method, he says. It's important in life to shoot for the extremes.

He never talks like this, thinks Jean. His head was never so cuboid.

PARK STREET

The kids get off. Atomize and reconstellate on the platform. The pets drift aft, others fore. Julie Bosko orbits.

Mr. Mulford leads them up rubber stairs. Unclimatized air, encrypted with smells: exhaust and sweetmeats. Cold. Everyone's breath steams. Brief suburban self-satisfaction is shared: they are in Boston on a weekday at ten. Mr. Mulford turns to Lusik, whispering, That was mostly for show, that bit. A *Blackboard Jungle* remake. You think they liked it?

I don't know, but your hair looked exceptional, says Lusik.

Mr. Mulford checks his not-quite-baldness. The pigeon on the PARK sign shows him one black eye. Are you coming on to me? Mr. Mulford asks it.

A vent tosses Jean's scarf skyward.

Jean, look out! says Peter. When it's windy do your parents keep you on a leash?

Peter, says Ugly. You're an idiot.

Honestly? he says. I'm depressed.

You don't look depressed, Ugly says.

Last night, Peter says, I dreamed I was being eaten alive by my hamster, Rob. He was doing it so slowly, it was more ticklish than painful, almost pleasurable, but still. Peter looks at Ugly meaningfully. Rob's been dead for *five years*.

Ugly sighs. You're not *depressed*.

Cloud cover muffles the sun. The kids play with their apertures, trailing Mr. Mulford south along the Common. Along Tremont, Mr. Mulford says, Stay close. A barbershop with one lathered man staring himself down in the mirror. No barber in sight. Lusik? says Jean. Him? She holds up her camera. Lusik shrugs. Her hair from behind is a wig falling off.

At Temple Place, Mr. Mulford says, Walk this way. Then he does the walk, arms limp, knees high, a Muppet fighting a wind. At school, the pets would copy, a classic, but not here.

At Boylston, they skirt the Combat Zone. Windows full of refurbished VCRs, the husks of strange squash. Down Washington the neon is sparse but fulfilling: NUD LIV GRLS. Belwick has no liquor license, let alone a red-light district. Julie Bosko takes aim, then turns back to flag the pets. Look.

She is pointing to a bakery window full of cakes variously bulbous and projectile, in many shades of pink and brown. One says, *Nothing Like a Piece of Ass* on one butt cheek and *Happy Birthday, Roberto* on another. There is a devil's food female torso with frosting bra and panties. There is *A Taste of Things to Cum* in curlicue script, and a male organ sheet cake iced in marzipan.

There is *Have a Balls of a Time, Herbert* with illustrative chocolate sprinkles.

Jean, how much to go inside? says Peter. He points out a cupcake. Five bucks to buy it. Ten to eat it.

Even the other pets have the notion that Jean is innocent to key facts. She got out of Mrs. Leary's Health Ed by writing a thirty-page paper about the human retina. She never even saw the woman's instructional banana. Jean would like to tell them all how much she refrains from revealing, but, in fact, she refrains from revealing very little.

She has not had the talk with her mother, because they do not have talks. Jean's mother in Jean's opinion has left the building. Take the bagged lunch: deviled ham for four days straight. This is patently remiss. Take Harvey: with Jane working overtime, no one walks him. The Bridges are roommates. Conversation beyond the instrumental deceased. At night everyone eats separately at a self-appointed hour on fold-out TV trays. The disbanding confuses Harvey, who attends each private meal in turn. Each diner feeds him scraps and he fattens.

Jean declares herself vegetarian. Repudiates the ham. Carries to school a single, obnoxious, demonstrative grapefruit.

THE GARDEN

At the corner of Charles and Boylston, the kids enter the Public Garden and gather by the lagoon where the Swan Boats dock. In an hour they will regroup here and head for the museum. Mr. Mulford suggests before parting that they consider the different fates of light. What becomes of it in water as opposed to dirt. Absorption, reflection, diffusion. How the color of a thing is not the light it holds but the light it rejects. How the eye understands not absolute wave forms but relative values. How turquoise next to blue is green, but next to green is blue. How to the eye *pure* white means nothing. Does not exist. And don't leave the Garden and don't get abducted. Abductees flunk. One hour sharp, back here, by the gate.

Smurf would like to make photographic puns—ladies holding gourds at chest level. Where are these ladies? Is it too cold for a farmers' market?

Art is not Ugly's elective, but she is here at the dispensation of Mr. Mulford, who likes her. She might zoom tight in on a flower, although it is inarguable what Lusik says, that nature, on close inspection, is boring.

Lusik loves Mr. Mulford but finds the medium tired. *The art of the art of the photograph. Dialectical nostril hair. I have a fun idea, Sontag: shut the fuck up. And take off that ridiculous wig.*

Jean is counting on the higher wisdom of Lusik for help with ions and with this. Jean has a hand, but Lusik has an eye.

A bearded vendor cries, What I have here will change your life! He hoists a squirt bottle. Smurf buys his pretzel. It is the size of her head and she holds it to her face like a mask while Ugly takes the shot. Lusik takes the pretzel from Smurf, accepts a squirt from the man. She chews then says a word to him in her own language. He nods.

What did you say? Julie Bosko asks from nowhere, through a mouth of fried dough.

Lusik walks away from the group, looking for a bench. She wants to finish her letter.

Lusik?

Lusik does not turn. I told him his mustard has made me an honest woman.

That's funny, says Julie.

Julie, says Lusik.

Sorry, says Julie. Lusik stops short and Julie bumps into her back. Sorry!

Lusik turns to face her. You apologize too much, she says. You apologize, you apologize, and then everyone has to forgive you. Don't you realize how selfish that is?

Ducks spill around them, closing them off from the pets.

No, says Julie. I don't.

She stands blinking in the weak sun. Her camera tucked there.

You know what we should do, says Lusik.

THANK YOU FOR NOT FEEDING US

Ugly and Smurf are throwing pretzel pellets at swans, against the signed policy, laying plans against mothers. Ugly's mother's muscles eat themselves, and she grows imperial. Would rule Ugly's body, tax its intake. For Ugly's sixteenth birthday, her mom gave her *Jesus's Diet for You,* a book of inspirational rhyme and verse to *supplement your weight-loss plan with a diet of God's Word.* Ugly is hoping to be an atheist. She enjoys Hermann Hesse. She exchanged *Jesus's Diet* for *The Glass Bead Game.*

Tomorrow after school, the pets will go to Ugly's and cook things that look like other things. Beets like gray-tailed mice, carrot soup like puke. Last week they baked bar cookies by the hundreds: apricot, lemon, hermit, brownie, and whatever provoking thing Lusik could make with all that was left over. What are *those?* Ugly's mom was alarmed. The cookies of my people, Lusik told her.

Smurf's mom has the voice of a female impersonator and eight languages she never speaks. It is the neighbors' favorite fact: eight languages to spare, imagine. Noam Chomsky hooking as Julia Child. But she throws nothing out and lets no one in the house to see. Only Smurf sees. Trash creeping everything. Tuna tins rank and crusted. Junk mail chin high snitched from others' stoops. And excessive cats: six. The cats are heliotropes, their bodies a sickening sundial. The house has no clock. You tell the time by the array of cat on rug.

Tomorrow is trash day. To Smurf's, at dawn, the pets will bring trash bags. They will meet Smurf at the door, smuggle it out, drive it for pickup to their own homes.

Jean stands off by the well-groomed hydrangeas, giving room to Smurf and Ugly for what is theirs alone by rights. Jean's parents are not ill, not reproachable. They are fit as fiddles and kind. Jean's mother is a kind and healthful mannequin impersonating the mother she was the first eight years of Jean's life, it is clear. Then something hatched. She defected. She went to school and took a job as an addiction counselor for homeless teens, of which she was once one, Ruth claims. Now she conducts her real life at a halfway house, with teens who know her deeply, teens suffering withdrawal and violation, not problem skin and a lynch mob in leg warmers.

Jean agrees to the trash help. But she cannot bake tomorrow. She has planned to study chemistry with Lusik after school.

Get her to help you today instead, says Ugly. My mom's home tomorrow and I want to do it while she's there.

Where did Lusik go? Jean says.

Off to write her letter, says Smurf. Tell her to hurry up. We need fried dough.

THE GOOD SAMARITAN

Jean follows the pond path, checking benches for Lusik.

SHADBLOW says a stake label. Is horticulture interesting? Jean does not know. She is less artist than camera herself, good only for replicating. A camera wielding a camera—what art can come of that? Jean lacks discrimination and knows it. Some don't even though: the Julies.

Consistently terrible photos would at least show discrimination. Shoot for the extremes. On the lookout for Lusik, Jean moves. Shoots tourists shooting tourist things. Equestrian George Washington. The world's second-smallest suspension bridge. MAKE WAY FOR DUCKLINGS in bronze and make sure to crop them badly. She crops tourist foreheads, the most photogenic of their children. She asks permission first and plays the small-person card and no one says no. Still no Lusik. Jean finds a tour group at a defunct fountain and gobbles through her film. Atop the fountain a statue honors not a person but a chemical: TO COMMEMORATE THAT THE INHALING OF ETHER CAUSES INSENSIBILITY TO PAIN. The turbaned and bearded *Good Samaritan* holds a pretty man across his knee, naked but for the drapery diaper so popular with sculptors.

On the Beacon side of the Garden, the light is doing something else. Refracting? Ornamental trees pay out into scabby elms. A new density of shrub, taller grass. The old marsh reclaiming.

Jean sees a solo tourist behind a quince and before she can ask for his photo, the man startles. No pictures, he says. It's for school, Jean says. No kidding, he says. Your fly, she says as he leaves.

Behind a viburnum Jean finds a man on a bench who smells of pomade and stares fixedly ahead. I'm looking for someone, says Jean. She does not raise her camera. You're on the wrong side, sister, he says.

Behind a mock orange is Julie Bosko on the ground. Gone is her shirt and bra. She is laid out there on her back with her hands behind her head, gazing at the sky too intently, like someone straining to hear a distant and improbable lyric. Julie, says Jean. Julie does not seem to hear. Julie, have you seen Lusik? Julie does not respond. Still the stare but pained. The nipples are finger thick, scab in color. Jean comes closer.

Bridges!

From behind, Jean's last name hits her. She turns and there is a crew-cutted man, squatting with a camera. Do you mind? You're in my light, says the man with Lusik's widow's peak. And it is Lusik, and Jean knows this, with a special sick lightness. The moment of free fall when your insides and outsides move at different rates. Jean understands physics.

You shaved your hair, says Jean, and hears the accusation, bereft and dumb.

Julie says, The barber did it.

Can I help you with something, Jean? says Lusik. Do you have five million questions I can answer for you? Wait, I have a fun idea—let's study for chemistry *right now*.

On the path back to the lagoon is Peter.

How much did you say to buy it, not eat it? asks Jean.

What? says Peter.

Astronaut lightness. Giddy-sick weightlessness. If she flip-turned off a tree she could zip to the gate, airborne. The two-facedness of inertia. *A body in motion*, she thinks, like a physicist. *Whatever you do, commit*, she thinks, like a lame motivational speaker. Two photos left. She floats without friction out of the Garden, retracing their route up Tremont. She passes over the bakery the first time. Backtracks. Surveys the display. The cupcake is gone. Pull the door, *ding-a-ling*. No one behind the counter. The sun plants rhomboids across checkerboard floor tiles. Is that interesting? Jean considers the cakes in the window: Is Roberto loved? For whom does Herbert yearn? The biggest by far is the marzipan sheet cake. Jean tests its weight. Four feet? Just inches shorter than she is tall. She balances it across her arms so that all the perimeter cocks are level. Moves slowly, pivots to open the door arms-free, and there behind the counter watching is the man who must have stood up from a squat, very quietly, very interested. All her Bridges cousins are cops with unruffled affects and taxidermy hobbies, and that is how he looks. Like his specialty is roadkill—he doesn't go after it, just takes what comes. He does not speak. Leans forward on his elbows, brows up, if not rapt then invested, like she is a play he has paid admission to and might as well see to the end. She backs her way out. Neither say a word. *Ding-a-ling.*

Jean flouts the crosswalk. Make Way for Cocklings. She floats across the street, barge steady, and cars stop, as they must. Back down Tremont, past the vendors, through the gate. Her forearms tremble. The smallest cock topples. She heads for the lagoon. She picks a patch of even ground, free of duck shit, and does a slow-motion plié to settle the cake. She rights the fallen one. Steps back until the frame contains it. Mr. Mulford was right. Colors are different by water. She steps back again, seeking proper vantage through the camera. Time is running out. Jean takes her shot.

She arrives at the gate appointed for the class to meet. She wants the pets so she can tell what she has done. Jean is not musical. But something syncopated and percussive is testing the small acoustics of her heart. All her liquid insides move in splendid concert. She feels her blood press its walls. She feels the vasodilation response. She perceives her skull spread. She feels her face disordered by feelings.

She looks for the pets.

She looks for Mr. Mulford.

She looks for Peter Hunig.

The sun dips, and with each drumbeat of her heart the light it offers dies.

She would welcome the sight of Julie Bosko.

The trees, her seniors by centuries, as a chorus inform her: Everyone has left without her. Everyone makes her way alone.

The nearest person at hand is the squirt vendor. Jean is determined not to run. She takes her time getting there, but still, when she reaches him, cannot quite locate the words.

Do you have the time? she says.

The man mimes no watch.

Did you happen to see a group of kids gathered by the gate?

The man waves off a pigeon.

Can you tell me which stop is the ICA?

The man will not look at her.

Jean hears in a loop Lusik's mom in her own language calling Lusik to the phone, announcing the persistent fact of Jean. But what exactly does she say? Lusik will never tell her.

The feelings jellify to one object, singular, without logic or origin. Jean is the object's host, not author. It spurns homeostasis. It follows strict Newtonian principles. It is solid but plastic and takes any number of shapes. It is a black scrim descended, a teeter-totter held down by an outsized guest, a funnel into which the bead of dark thoughts spirals irretrievably down.

Once before, it visited Jean. She never told the pets. To the basement Jean carried it and there placed a call to a suicide hotline. It was that night, as the line rang with gross deliberation, that she saw her mother pass, a shadow edging out of the basement laundry room, in a seahorse bathrobe smelling of smoke. Later Jean found the butts secreted behind the washer. That night Jean and Jane did not acknowledge each other. They looked at each other like criminals.

Now, Jean tries Lusik's mother's words to Lusik, phonemes familiar and strange, out loud once and quietly.

95

The vendor's face breaks.

The light glances off it in a new way and cracks it. A molecular rupture and the face becomes visible to Jean not as a face but as a landscape you might penetrate through any of several ports of entry, eyeholes, noseholes, earholes, mouth. In the mouth is a pebbled tongue. Jean can sense it awake in its hot cavity, mollusk testing air. Somewhere on the other side of the cart is the man's lower half and it too welcomes her and if she walks around the cart it is conceivable she could embrace it, eye to navel, possess and lift it off the ground.

how did they meet?

6

LES MIS

Woonsocket, 1976; Fourchu, 1919; Boston, 1924

FOR THE SUNDAY RIDE TO NANA D.'S AND AUNT ESTHER'S JANE
brought an anxious lot of sugar. The interstate to Woonsocket
took one hour. To Jean and Ruth, Jane passed back Tastykakes or
Devil Dogs or Yodels or Yoohoos or Ding Dongs or Dum Dums
or powder puff doughnuts. The girls accepted these stipends without appetite. Everything with a soft white surprise in the center.

Or else foods that you could make things out of. Licorice ropes
an armspan long and filament thin that the girls knotted into
chain-gang anklets.

What Jean and Ruth liked best were the turnips. Jane stopped
at Sunnyhurst Farm just past the state border. The turnips were
vegetable outlaws, special spawn of Rhode Island, exotic in the
proud and debased way of that state. They tasted good and barely
edible. Fun to eat, like eating a chair. Jane picked out a dozen—
purple grading to yellow and more solid than apples. Propped on
the hood she skinned each with a pocket knife. From the blade
sprang one continuous skein that Ruth telescoped back to a shell of
a turnip, a black joke on turnips. Jane sliced the flesh up into slick

fat coins. The coins perspired starch and were for biting designs into. Jean bit hers into moons. Ruth bit hers into frowns that were moons and copycats of Jean's. Invention for Ruth was a kind of trouble. At the rest stop Jane bit hers into a three-story house using her eyeteeth for windows and widow's walks and sleep-in porches. *Save it!* said Ruth and Jean. *Give it here!* they said and they pleaded *shellac it and make it an ornament*, but Jane chewed it up, smiling with metal-packed teeth.

It would just go bad if I did, she said.

Jane's teeth were crafty but her hands were famous. Until the girls walked she sewed all of their clothes. She knit mittens that doubled as puppets. Bent coat hangers into halos and wire-frame wings and wove yarn wigs for Halloween—how the other mothers fumed. For Ruth's sixth birthday she constructed an angel-food castle with a chocolate drawbridge operated by widget. Boiled lollipops for stained glass. Oh my, said the other mothers when their girls told of it. The basement was feral. Plastic paneled and ceilinged in scabietic pipes—its ugliness inspired Jane. From those pipes swung unoccasioned piñatas of newsprint dredged in flour glue. The girls' guests clubbed them. Also from the pipes was Jane's gift-o-matic. The girls' guests drew numbers. They tugged a corresponding string that dangled and worked a pulley that let down a gag gift—a calico frog stuffed with lentils. Jane sewed, stuffed, and rigged it.

Once a month, at Building 19, laserlike in that headache hangar, Jane pawed the priced-to-move ends of fabric bolts.

She made Italian ice with a hammer and syrup.

Any day of the week, any guest of the girls would not leave giftless.

The girls' guests loaded up in a bewildered frenzy.

Jean and Ruth could give no explanation. They said of Jane only, She likes to do it.

Your mother can make anything out of anything—this from the other mothers, who knew Jane from the distance of the uncrossed yard. The mothers waved from the car when dropping off or collecting. When Jane spoke to them, it was by phone in the kitchen with her back to Jean. It was about when to drop off and when to collect. With stagey gestures—fending off favors or gnats.

Jean watched these calls in the crossed-arm pose of a cop.

After, Jane would say, That woman buys six-packs of underwear when her maid goes on vacation. A medical doctor who can't operate a washer.

Or sometimes, mad: What are you looking at?

Jean's mother never cried.

Her sister never cried.

Her father never lied.

Jean lied sometimes and cried often, so strong-lunged and bestial that Jane could do nothing but close her in a cold shower clothed. She got Jean in fast with those fast-thinking hands—the way she crushed spiders or plucked out teeth.

For Ruth, the trouble was not crying but wiseness.

Don't get wise with me, Jane said, and it was not water to cure it but a slap to the face. She was slapping her own was the feeling you got.

Ruth took it and walked, uncured. Like she had appointments in that house to keep.

In her lonesome immunity, Jean held her own hands.

In the car to Woonsocket, Jane told a story about an orphan girl adopted by a thieving man. In the story, everyone poor was good and French. The best ones died of galloping consumption. Jean assumed it was the story of Jane's life. Assumed this although they were on the road to Jane's still-breathing parents. When Jean was grown she said as much to Ruth—remember how Mom used to tell us her life on that drive?

It was Ruth's burden to be right (which came down to being attentive and unforgetting). By its inattention and forgetfulness the world contrived to pain her. She lodged her complaint by keeping her voice low. At her most right and pained, Ruth was an alto. In that low way she said to Jean, That was the plot of *Les Misérables*. You know it. You've seen it. We saw it together.

Jean felt ill then with theft—felt that someone had seized, with legal warrant, what she had wrongfully owned.

Tell it again, said Jean and Ruth in the car as soon as Jane finished, but Jane always said, I can't. We're here.

Woonsocket was danceable.

You could feel it: a committee of adults colluding to please you, for reasons that preceded you and were certainly not you. Your pleasure, it was clear, was the outcome of a treaty.

Woonsocket was cigarettes and fudge, dogs and dress pins.

The fudge was undercooked, the dogs frenetic.

The dress pins were rhinestone ladybugs set on felt velveteen, and Nana D. would show them shyly and sometimes give them up.

You ate until your stomach was a pendulum and its upswing toppled you.

The neighborhood had the lying-low breathing of the recently bullied. You sensed the triumphal exit of earth movers. The land had no features but crowfoots and newts.

The houses on Nana and Esther's street looked like the town you'd make, bored, with old school milk cartons. Like every fifth on the street, their house siding was mint.

And behind it: old persons, the significant ones fitting in ready-grin teeth the moment that Jane killed the engine out front.

Guess who ruined the fudge! Nana D. greeted them this way. We'll eat it with spoons.

She stood back-to-back with Ruth and beat her by only inches.

That grin as athletic and jazzed-out as a tap dance. Nana did somersaults on command. That's enough, said Jane. Let Nana D. be.

Charming Nana!

Attached to a cigarette was the other old person of note, Aunt Esther, with a bullfrog's mesmeric perseverance and register—stay stay stay stay STAY—and attached to her by that leash of voice were three Boston terriers. They speed-skated linoleum. They dropped glutinous plumb lines of spittle. Esther's hands took turns, one on cigarette detail and one off duty interred in a pot of shea butter.

Be good, Special, or I'll put you down, my love. Esther said this to her favorite, Someone Special, and then her bones, slip stitched in khaki veins, shuddered.

Jane and Nana would cry, Don't laugh, don't laugh!

Esther laughed as one giving out.

After, she'd have to lie in the bedroom and hook up to the tank.

The oxygen tank with tattling sighs reinflated her.

Jean and Ruth fitted soupspoons of fudge in their mouths.

Woonsocket was one marathon baptism.

It was as if Jane could not bear to see them there dry. Like it was her mission to liquefy all points of contact.

Woonsocket was a slugfest of low-rent water fun: hose, sprinkler, wading pool, bath.

With the hose and sprinkler you turned the scant apron of backyard to slaphappy mud.

In the pool you drowned newts you mistook for aquatic.

In the bath, you machined products. You conducted science. Every cream, lotion, shampoo, and shaving soap pestled to paste and rolled into straight-to-market beauty pellets, gray from your skin, whose benefits you evangelized hard to Nana D. Close your eyes and just *feel* this, you'd say, and snail the pellet down the loose sleeve of her arm skin.

Ooo! she'd say, the easy mark, but sometimes too soon. You'd have to scold her.

Gramp was a sweatered installation in a La-Z-Boy knockoff. His hue was tobacco. The chair was balding, the sweater misbuttoned. If it weren't for the eyes and hands, you would think him asleep. The fingernails were claw thick and injurious as weevils. They worried the armrests, found loose thread and pulled. The skull was fixed on its axis and handsomely armed in a spring-loaded pompadour. Inside the eyes swiveled. They saw people as columns of darkness moving in with agendas to part him from that which he still held rights to, that chair. They saw dogs as avengers. The eyes were watchdogs for dogs and alerted the hands. When a dog entered the room, one hand leapt up to puppeteer a mouth.

Gramp's hand growled. It nipped the air. The nails of it gnashed.

Feel lucky? Gramp said.

Someone Special skated backward.

Every bath was a plenary session. Esther rested, but Nana and Jane attended. While Ruth took hers, Jean moved in on Gramp with a spoonful of fudge.

Open up, she said.

She held the spoon to the mouth. With one fervent hand she parted the lips. The teeth within were his last defense.

Open up, you pickleworm, she said.

The self-acting hand on the armrest tensed. In Gramp things roiled. Kicked up a bad sediment.

Telepathic Esther, hooked up out of view, knew. Stay stay stay! she called from her bedroom. Thrush, you stay or I'll put you down!

Jean put down the spoon.

Gramp's eyes beheld the sun-stroked yard with speculation.

Feel lucky? Gramp said. Soon the white stuff will be coming down.

Why does he always say that? said Ruth in the hall. It's June.

Jean watched Gramp's eyes roll to show their white backs.

Keep luck on her toes. Make her feel lucky. You said that. Your skin was gone that skim-milk blue. May I never drink milk. You said luck must like my looks, me hanging on, unfevered, so keep her. The blood wormed thickly out of your ears. Stained the ticking. The wild dogs outside were numerous, plunderous, rooting the earth where I buried Hank. They let out moans like humans rutting. May I never feed a dog. March of '19 was the Spanish flu. Every door in Fourchu marked out for quarantine, a wet tar X in the hand of that pink-eyed Halifax officer. Fourchu occupants jailed to their sick house. But lobster would not haul themselves— get what's ours before it's got, you said. So we got out and got it. Now the March earth hard and Hank dug too shallow. You yelled to dig your grave deeper from the sickbed window. Stand in it and let me see how deep. I want to see just the rims of your eyes. The ground was hard and I was tired. I was twelve. Eleven graves, one for every year I'd kept on. This my first to dig alone. Yours will be my last, I thought. So I crouched. I cheated. You see me, I called, it's up to my eyes! May I never have to sweat to eat. A tip, you said: Pay luck no mind, then pay her mind when she's given up. When her value's down. Buy low, you said. Timing is all. How do I pay luck mind? I said. Me twelve and you sixteen, my last and my least. Your lungs two sets of lips gummed and smacking. Two drowning mouths inside your chest. Smack smack. It made me ill. The sound of me overboard that once, just us two. I was eight. Ma just passed and Da long gone. I was drowning before you. You docked the oars in the wherry and studied me. Your eyes an odd annunciation. Some new truth: paler than I knew. I scrabbled for the surface, beat the water with my fists. Try harder, you said. Try harder, you said. You stabbed the oar at my hand on the corkline. I pawed the tumblehome. You rowed from reach. The waters swallowed me. They had taught you swimming this way too. Chester taught you and Lloyd taught Chester and Tom taught Aubrey taught Donald taught Hank taught Fred taught Cyril taught Clint taught Lloyd. The water closing its cold throat above me. Light spilling down, a shafting liquid. I beat through that to air and saw in your eyes that you did not like me. Indifferent eyes. Not blue blue but skim-milk blue. May I never drink milk; may I never be beholden to one who never liked me; may I ever be a gift to the one who does. To spite you, my lungs on the spot grew feathery gills. I went amphibian. I kicked away from you and straight for the bottom and lay there amid soft and soundless decay for three nights straight. I chewed on substrate. I became a bottom-feeder. A human lobster. And when I returned to that house, you could no longer touch me.

Then I was twelve, unfevered, and it was your turn to feel death upon you. Gag up blood yolks in the bucket I held. What you had left was an hour maybe. You were drowning on blood, my last blood kin, who never liked me, and the last order you gave was the one I did not keep: Dig me deeper than Hank. If you let the dogs eat me, I'll kill you myself.

If you could you would. But the dead can't kill.

The wild dogs ate you five feet before me and yet I breathe.

I quit Fourchu.

What I did, I joined the rummies.

The Boston Rum Row syndicates are onetime banana boats, battered beam trawlers, tramps, schooners, bankers, yachts, all rust-faced fugitives from the knacker's yard. Swivel's freelance. He's got an ex-navy subchaser. He rides it at anchor five miles offshore. The syndicates unload faster and funner—call girls board who double their shoreside price, a hazard bonus is what they call it—but Swivel's dependable. He pays the go-through decent.

I'm seventeen and a go-through man. My little flat-bottom skiff I call *Tortoise*. Never show your cards in a name. Her payload is fifty cases. She docks in the mudflats, down past the busted molasses tank. Flea sedge and spike rush give good cover.

Sundown, I pull out with the sunset fleet. Go-through jobs sprung from hidden coves zip across the three miles of U.S. territorial. I move with them at twenty-five knots. Hail the mother ship. Pull alongside. Pay off the supercargo. Load to the gunwales. Wave to the Coast Guard revenue cutters: Spanish-American War relics with coffee-grinder engines straining flat out to make ten knots. Designed for iceberg patrol is what they are. The poop-along ladies. They count tonnage, wave back, sleepy.

At the landing point, the Stateside agent's there with his convoy. His work gang unloads. His gunmen smoke and suck cream from éclairs.

Here's the math: Swivel buys up Scotch for eight dollars a case at St. Pierre; sells it off Rum Row for sixty-five to the agent who sells it to bootleggers for one hundred and thirty. Landed price is at least double. Now, shoreside bootleggers doctor it three to one, turn around the eight dollar case for four hundred. National

Aridity is a regular wet nurse. She suckles the good and the bad alike. Even the Coast Guard men in their picket boats score—it's promotions and promotions, a gravy train.

It doesn't even take luck. If you were a fisherman yesterday, today you're a rummy.

For one year straight, everyone's happy.

But spring of '24, the Coast Guard and Congress make a resolution about balls. How they adore them and want to grow some. They get ideas. Idea number one is to push back the Rum Line from three miles to twelve—thinking to put the Row out of reach of us small craft. Some, it's a fact, can't do the distance. But *Tortoise* is tight as ticks. Idea number two is hire on Swedish merchant seamen named Lars, their two words of English yes and put-put. Idea three: Take twenty-five destroyers out of retirement. Thousand tonners, moving at thirty knots. Mounted one-pounders for close-in work. These take station at mile twelve, to breathe down hard on the necks of Rum Row. And behind them at intervals the bad news for go-throughs: flotillas of six bitters and picket boats. Shoreside sand pounders haunt the beaches.

Now luck counts. So I make luck want it. I go bold. Push *Tortoise* harder. Go after dark, cloud cover, no lights, trust luck to steer us shy of sandbars. Those who woo luck wrong get boarded. Too much sissy foot unmans you for luck. If you're outward bound, tossing salt over shoulders and twiddling hare foots, cutters will surely find fault with your life vests. They'll ask for documents. They'll take two hours to analyze handwriting.

God likes the bow and scrape. He cuts deals for toadies. Well, I dance swell, but not on my knees. I take instead luck. Luck is a call girl who likes my looks and my steps. Sometimes a slap. But sometimes all that fatigues a man. Here was my misstep running go-through for Swivel. I became too cozy. I drank up the days, dillydallied my runs. I misread the weather. One day in June I saw them: clouds banked up against the sky, green-gray, sun showing as through a film of ground glass. Wrong clouds for *Tortoise*. *Tortoise* hates snow. I foresaw the snow, but who would believe it—it's June, you fool, I told myself. I discounted the clouds and drank my cut brew. I stewed off the day. But the light filtering down through cloud cover blurred me, and, like a fool, when at sundown I pushed out I by accident prayed. Pleasebetogodletthepissfuckingsnow-holdoff. To what in hell was I praying? No matter. I two-timed luck. And for that one day, luck didn't want me.

The waves are steep at mile twelve and snow comes hard as Swivel's men hand down the last case. On your mark, the revenue cutters. They skulk up, lights off, tonguing your way, lappity lap lap, and you might think it's fish. You might think big game. But it's not halibut. It's picket boat. Swivel signals it. And me already loaded up fifty case. Cut the engine, Swivel says. Give the wheel a turn to port and lash it, says he. Lappity lap lap. Lappity lap. And the cutter closes in and then pisses off. Nothing. Hoopla.

Trouble is, I've drifted. Can't see for snow. And the engine, overloaded from a dead start, labors. I'm misdirected in bad sea, shoved headwise to Swivel. Twenty footers and my prow blowing Swivel's stern. The blessed romance of it. A row of pale patches where the faces of Swivel's men glow watching from the subchaser deck, immovable. The air hurts. My engine won't catch. Then the hit. Glancing, and my pilothouse lays out sideways. The rail swoons starboard, buckled down flat to deck. By the moon—it's high—about two ante meridiem. Not a good hour.

Nor the worst. If the wave had hit any sooner I'd have nailed the counter of the subchaser square and been gone. Instead I beat death to the punch and dove.

To all eyes I disappeared for good. The water took me.

But did luck take me back, a lobster?

You judge.

I drifted the bottom for three nights straight.

It was so soft down there and so soundless.

I was a goddamn peaceful crustacean.

When I at last surfaced, I met luck herself. She had taken the body of a flat-chested kid. Younger than I thought and a good deal odder. She touched my cheeks like they were flesh, not shell. She laid her body on mine like ours were one body. So close was she, my eyes could not converge to see her. She doubled before me. When she spoke, I could not say from whose mouth the words came: I paid for you and you're mine to keep.

Drink hulled Gramp's brain. When Jean was grown, Jane spoke of how Nana was going to put Gramp in a home, but Esther said keep him for the pension check. Wasn't it Nana's house, her say? asked Ruth. Jane said it was not. The house was Esther's, Eddy's when he lived, willed him by Alice. Thrush would have hated nothing more than to know he lived off Eddy's good graces.

Soon the piss-fucking white stuff will be coming down.

As if to back him, Gramp's eyes showed only their whites.

Nana D. came in from the bathroom and stood before him. When Nana's hand touched his cheek, Jean saw him shiver.

what remains?

7

FEVER DOGS

➤➤ Holyoke, 1923; Boston, 1924 ◄◄

When, in a man's hand, the finger of Jupiter is short and
crooked, the first phalange of the thumb heavy, and the
second phalange poor, the lower mounts over-developed,
the Heart-line short and without branches—it would be
well not to marry that person.

—E. RENÉ, *HANDS AND HOW TO READ THEM*

BOSTON IS A CLUB-FINGERED SPATULATE HAND. MAPS SHOW THIS.
Mother says: If the city were a man, he would do best to be a butcher.

Esther does not want to go seaward. Water is to die in, to extract
your sins or punish them. If you're runty, drown in a sack. If you're
weepy, wet your head. Nothing like cold water down your collar
to dry your eyes. Esther and Doris eat no fish, just fries with curd
and gravy Fridays. Holyoke has one algae-slick pond like a diges-
tive tract. This is Shrike. Whatever you toss in it is gone, juiced.
Both Esther and Doris were baptized in that pond by a blind itin-
erant deacon who was later exposed as a Methodist and sighted.
He was caught wearing glasses two towns over. Before baptizing,

he tongued their nostrils languorously, so that they would know the odor of God.

The parish men who found him removed his glasses. They removed his eyes with pliers before they tossed him in Shrike.

Esther and Doris do not swim. Both their left-hand Luna mounts are grilled with small lines. On each a bad star. In this they are alike, and Mother says: Luna mounts like that make you unsafe for water.

Yet Esther's right hand is her own to write, and west of Holyoke are just more pulp mills and cows. Busybody parishes. Waitressing and strangers to Esther sound good. When consumption takes Mother, Esther sells off the last old animals. She takes Doris east. Fearing damp, they ride the Boston–Albany line ninety miles wearing every piece of clothing they own. They look like laundry. Woolen capuches rash their foreheads red. Each balances on her knees a lurching *tourtière* that neither can stomach to eat or to part with. In Esther's pillowcase: E. René and underwear. In her boot, egg money. At the end of the line, their laps stink of pork.

What they find is a brackish city. Boston waging a grudge match with sea. It lops off its hills to soak up its ponds. It dams its mudflats to shore up a river. A fingered mass flattening out to gain ground. Twice a day the tide retreats and children scavenge the defunct mill sluice for shells, hoops, coins, bones.

Beyond South Station a dock extends in a scarf of fog. Up flap gulls and beanied men shout. Bowsprits crosshatch the far-off blue.

A man docks a dory. He has a pepperbox and cruet and says, Come and get it. He has no legs. The empty dungarees fill and fall like lungs. He sorts a mound of deformed rocks in a crate beside him and knives his selection and twists the blade and administers vinegar and pepper while Doris stares. He inserts the split stone in his mouth and throws back his head. Oysterman, says the station newsboy. Across the street gapes a hole in the ground big enough to consume a house. A guard in a jumpsuit waves off traffic. Subway expansion, says the boy. Irish tunnel under at night, he says. Try the South End, he says when Esther and Doris do not move.

Bostonians would conceive rivers out of marsh, then ride trains beneath them as if rivers were conceptions.

And as you walk the tracks south, people do not see you, like you are a thing not yet conceived. This suits Esther. Humid air hits her face like fresh plaster. She strips off a coat, an apron, a sweater. Five-story walk-ups sag and go provisional, revert from stone to brick to wood at Fort Hill.

Doris says experimentally, I hate it here.

I like it, says Esther. Doris, a poor but jealous eater, will hunger for anything on Esther's plate. In this way Esther tricks Doris into appetite, and in the same way she will trick Doris into good faith.

Doris hangs off Esther's arm and plucks at the tender skin above the elbow. When Esther says that hurts, Doris checks her own skin for bruises. Esther finds herself checking Doris too.

Aren't you hot? says Doris and spits. I'm hot. Is that interesting? Doris is a prodigious spitter.

Keep Doris close, Mother had said.

Doris carried a screwdriver. At night she lifted pretty bits of hardware off parish doors for a month. Sunday, she gave those to Shrike. If she fed it, it would feed her.

Out of Shrike rose a hound.

The hound broke the pond's green mantle, swam a line to Doris, climbed ashore, and shook free a thick suit of algae. Its skin was furless, the pink caul of an infant. Mother was born wearing her caul, a silly hood. It gave her her second sight. She wore it around her neck in a pouch.

That the hound followed Doris home was no surprise. It followed her anywhere. It wanted only to be close. As they walked, Doris held the low bowers of tamaracks so that they would not beat the hound's half-made flesh.

Doris called the hound Deacon.

The lodging house lady asks if Doris is Esther's child. Doris is five years younger! But also a foot shorter and that catenary noodle of a body looking always on the verge of a fit or a jig, whereas Esther is tall and hinged, deliberate. When Esther says no, the lady says good.

Days Esther does dish duty in a canteen for boys studying law. Another red-brick box larded white past the Fens. The basement scullery is swampy. A communicating dumbwaiter takes the dirty things down to it. Two for one, Esther says to the Bridget who hires her, because she can see that the woman thinks Doris too young. Doris is young, a too-young twelve. Aging skittishly, forward and backward. But where else can Doris go all day? Doris sweeps, Esther says, and buses tables and sticks by me—that last part true. Doris herds Esther. Doris sweeps but forgets her sweepings. Abandoned anthills of bread crumb and gristle. One day, she breaks two plates dancing some kind of reel. The other day girl, Irma, adjusts her hairnet. Pits caked in orange pock her cheeks, and she has a habit of hiding by not meeting your eyes. Let me finish, will you, whispers Esther to Doris. Go up and clear the last tables. Don't talk to anyone. Doris leaves, her pliable face gone flat.

The room falls wordless. Steel and stoneware and stuck bits of forcemeat. Bird jelly scums Esther up to the wrist. As she rinses the last spoon, something like applause spills down the shaft in a current. Esther goes up. There in the dining hall is Doris, three sweet buns in her mouth and cramming another. A small circle of aspiring lawyers in cufflinks holding out spares. Doris spits out bun bits, gags, swallows, and says to her audience, Also, I juggle.

Esther collars Doris. Downstairs she says, You really went for it, didn't you. Irma has gone. Esther raises her hand to smack her sister. She has never hit anyone. She has wanted to, often. Now the mechanics of it stump her. Her arm goes pins and needles. Blood pools at the elbow. I'm tired is the thing, she says. Her arm lowers and her eyes shut to enable recollection of trees that she knows by sight—white oak blackjack hemlock pine chinaberry pecan mockernut hickory—then open at a watery clap. Doris stands drenched. Her hand holds an empty glass. Water travels her chin to the puddle she stands in. Doris shakes her head, spraying droplets like a very wet dog. She looks surprised.

Doris says, They gave us these, and pulls from her right pocket a nickel, a matchbook, and a broken potpie.

Doris keeps to herself what was not given: two enamel cufflinks backed in gold.

Doris lifted scrap from her plate to feed Deacon.

She slept with Deacon locked in embrace.

They were the same height precisely.

When Mother took to bed with fever, she spoke to Doris of fever dogs. Pour some milk in a bowl and let the dog drink it. Then the fevered person drinks. Back and forth goes the bowl. When the milk is gone, the person is cured.

And the dog? said Doris.

Mother said that every death needed a home. She said that Deacon would house her death, as Mother had housed him.

Before dawn Doris led Deacon to Shrike. She told him go. He would not go. Weeping, from her pocket she drew five stones. She threw them

in order smallest to biggest, first at his feet, then at his shank. Deacon
would not go. The fifth was the size of his head and aimed for it. Dea-
con ran blind. Roots tripped him. Tree trunks fenced him. Until she
lost sight of him in the forest litter, Doris counted the blows his tender
skin took and for each extracted a hair from her head. She fed those to
Shrike. Shrike ate those, but hair is the body's practice death and what
is already dead cannot sate hunger.

Shrike said: More, more, more.

Doris gave Mother's bowl of milk instead to a barn cat. Deacon is
drinking, she misinformed her mother. Your turn next.

Esther and Doris prop the slatted chair beneath the doorknob and
undress to slips. On the sheets they print thin sweat selves. Doris
swats off Esther's comb. She chops at deerflies, robust and furred.
She lobs them like shuttlecocks with the flats of her hands. Esther
reads a chapter on tarot. With a steak knife she pares dead skin
from her heels. Doris dips her hand in a jar of molasses and suckles
each pointed finger in turn. Where did you get that? says Esther.
When do you get out alone?

Some blocks from the lodging house a fifty-foot molasses drum
leaks. From their window, they can see kids coming and going.
They ferry the tarish syrup in old chipped-beef cans.

Doris walks the plank of the bed to the end. Stiff as a stiff, she
drops. At the moment of collision she cinches up and rolls. Her
spine lashes the rag rug. Soon the lodging lady's broom end will
Morse code quit.

I wish I could be shot from a cannon into snow, says Doris from
the floor. It's hot.

Mother's chief worry for Doris derived from those fingers—
short and knotless like a religious fanatic's. The palms too are bad.
The heart lines islanded, and surmounting the bracelets are deep

lines of intemperance. Both hands show it. These things might be averted, but by Esther, not Doris. It was best if Doris did not know, Mother had said.

You're on my watch till you marry, thinks Esther. Doris wipes her gummy hand in her hair and works at contortion. She licks molasses off her fingers and works at second sight. Esther thinks, I will find you someone.

Doris thinks, You needn't. I will find my own.

The barn cat died.

But it was too small a home.

In her last week, Mother's cough went thready. She spoke to Esther of how when she died she might bring mischief upon them, as the dead were now bringing mischief upon her. Esther asked her what sort of mischief, and would she not, in death, to her capacity, mother them.

Mother's face was a hatchet in shape, a sponge to touch. Her breath smelled like meat.

Mother said, Look at me.

Mother said, Can't you see that I am being eaten? Can't you see that when dead I will eat you?

Mother said, When I die, dig out my heart. Burn it on a fire of sally twigs. If you do not, go away from here. Run far or not at all. My heart will hunt you and feed upon you.

Nights, while Doris sleeps, Esther gets into her Gypsy getup. She knots a shawl beneath her chin. She does her lips gash-red and bigger than life and runs a dozen bangles up one forearm. Until closing, she sits in the greasy window of the rail yard Forest Club that serves good chips and wretched pickled things—knuckles, eggs, baby onions, tongues. Her job is to lure. To detect and smile at money passing by. When money enters, she watches how it moves. She watches how it eats, and when it comes to her twitchy and hands rotating upward, she knows already half of what to say. She thickens the accent. None of them place it.

Few men come to her. The Forest Club men are there to be alone, communing and smoking and alone like each table is an adjoining stall and the place a kind of safe house for privacy, a public theater or toilet in which you can get fed. They do not look at her. She senses in the quality of that not looking fear. It comes to her that first night that her cheap costume has overshot the mark. No one sees her as seventeen or a girl. They see her as some grim reaper in drag. They see her as fate, their personal predator.

Those who do come have confession on their lips. They want the opposite of what a confessor gives. Whatever it is—and it is theft and betrayal, that's all, that's enough—they don't want forgiveness, do not believe in it. They want to know if they will be caught. They have concerns about cost. There is something groveling and abject in the way they cast their eyes about the floor and she finds herself repulsed and full of mercy. She cannot help them except by lying. In a lying style, she does not say the worst to them, faggots of lines and stars and crosses, withered Mercurys and crooked Saturns, but carries it home like a bad food ingested.

From two to six in the morning Esther tosses next to Doris and craves fresh boudin. Craves licking the bloody innards from the intestinal casing the way Doris would go at a sugar-pie whisk. Not hunger. Need like a splinter she can't stop poking. Their hallmate, the needlewoman, says it only gets worse. She says nothing cures it. She says not all the boudin in the world cures it.

At six Esther rises and fills their basin down the hall. She brings it back and sponge bathes while Doris grinds her face in a pillow.

Do you think it's hot out? Doris says.

The window right there for looking out of. A drugget shade stirs and sun stripes their feet.

To Doris, Esther says, I'm glad you asked, because there's no way of knowing. To herself, she thinks, I will find you someone.

You needn't, thinks Doris. I can find my own.

Nights, while Esther dresses to go, Doris half sleeps. She listens for the lodging-house door latch behind Esther then rouses too to dress and to earn. She has two hours to do exactly what she wants— enough to run six blocks through gaslight and chill to the molasses drum, to consume as much as her hands can collect. Three blocks more to the dead mill sluice, where small treasure can be had, unhindered by competition, and half a dozen more past the Fens to Muddy River. Muddy River is the mouth of the tidal flats and stinks—but is lucky in proportion to stink and generous in proportion to what she feeds it. Muddy River returns her the gifts of shipwrecks. One night she feeds it a canteen cufflink and within the hour receives from the effervescent mud below the rotten dock two mercury dimes and three peace dollars. For cufflink two, one week later, Muddy River returns three bottles of intact Canadian whiskey. She feeds it canteen forks, and it pays her in bottles. Beneath the rotten dock is a ledge to keep her take. Sedge grass hides it. When she has enough, she can discharge Esther of her night work and of Doris. Esther must be free to leave her. It is what Doris owes.

Esther's good luck is this: wide-spaced level straight conic fingers, unwaisted thumb, and a feathered heart line. Farsightedness with the right things. Speak of hawks, she can spot one miles off by its wingspan. A good man at twenty yards by his cranial geometry, and then, at close range, by his hands, she corroborates.

Whatever boldness made her come here was not foretold and not welcome in Holyoke. Esther willed it. Compare the Mars mound of her right hand to that of her left.

The day they buried Mother, the tamaracks acted as if Doris was strange. They made no way for her. They argued in whispers.

Doris wore Mother's gift in its pouch at her waist hidden between her apron and skirt. Mother had said, You need the second sight more than Esther will.

At Shrike, Doris loosened the pouch. She tipped out the gift. The caul was pink, the size of a prune. It looked to her just like a piece of Deacon. She took a small bite, swallowed, tossed the rest to Shrike.

The caul skated the green to the deepest middle but would not sink.

Then Shrike said, No.

Shrike said, I need what is needed.

Shrike said, I made him.

Doris said, If you don't want my caul, then give it back.

Shrike said, If you will not feed Deacon, give him back.

Esther had her back to the stove studying her hands when Doris returned wet to the waist. On the table was open the book Mother gave Esther.

The pot is boiling over, Doris said.

Esther moved it from the heat and looked at Doris. She did not ask why Doris was wet. She asked Doris what if we leave.

He is really something.

Esther first sees him passing her by, through glass. She knocks. She tents her eyes.

You want to talk to me, she mouths.

He walks a chicken-sized dog with fur like a tux and stands a head taller than the crowd but moves slow.

He stays the dog to look at her.

You want to talk to me, she mouths and signs.

He scoops up the dog.

Wrong man, he mouths back and keeps looking. Square hand, fingers equal in length to palm, big. Ring.

No, big doesn't cover it. Hands to bully oxen or uproot trees.

But two weeks after, he's at the nearest table ringless, paying her this compliment: Excuse me for saying it, but sister, you've had rotten luck.

Better than *what small*, *what white*, *what green*, what-have-you.

He says, What kind of rotten luck does it take for a girl like you to wind up here?

He has a quiet and hoarse sort of accent of his own. Like a person spent from yelling and now done. She hefts her clangorous left hand and says, If by luck you mean what you're dealt, that's this hand only. That's only the half of it.

His black eyes so wide set she has to favor one speaking. Buttressing cheeks and mansard nose. A shock of dark hair drains into the summit of his skull, which dimples profoundly, two handholds back of ears. Like his head is a thing to lug.

She says, I don't know your sister, but you look nothing like my brother.

Where's he? he says. A man shouldn't let his sister work a place like this.

I ditched him, Esther says. Wouldn't stop following me. Bossy, too.

The man says, I see.

His breath slow beneath crossed arms.

Who said I have a brother? Esther says. I have a sister, much nicer than me, and older than she looks. Esther plucks an ice cube from her tonic and draws a wet letter on her arm. She erases it slowly. Hey, where you from? Don't you have a dog? A real little lapdog, like the kind for a lady.

Esther likes to hurt people she likes, just a bit, to show them that she knows where their hurt lies. Pain is intimate and nice when withheld. What good is withholding if you don't show that you hold it.

That's the past, he says. You're billed here as some oracle.

Why do you think I'm here if not to meet you? she says.

He reangles the lamp head at her. A line, he says. How old are you anyway.

Open up, she says and holds one ice cube high. He does not open. Open, she says. He does not. Open and hurry, she says, I can't stay like this forever, my arm is sore enough to fall off right now. Where will that leave a girl like me? No one cares a fig for a one-armed girl.

He does not appear to move, but the next thing the ice cube is in his hand, not hers. Just like that.

Do you consider yourself a creative complainer? he says. He shakes his hand dry.

Don't look like that, says Esther. What good is that face? I read hands.

The next time he puts a chair opposite Esther and fits himself to it with his legs shot sideways in an attitude of waiting.

She continues reading the funny papers by a candle nub. She can read words, unlike Doris, but pictures tell more.

Hello, Eddy, she says. The pub owner has given her that much. His face is this immaculate platter, calmness sweeping it ear to ear. What it is is lack of strain. She feels more or less like an ant or rodent, tunneling for air. He has no shortage of air. It is not about height. Esther is tall. She says, I can't hear myself think with all your chatter.

When he does not answer, she says, What's that, you're concerned for my health? My feet hurt. Is that interesting? Not at all, no. You're in the mood for a joke. There's a woman and a doctor. The woman says my feet hurt and my tooth aches and sometimes my ear rings. Also this, she says and points to her face, not bad, rather ugly. Is that all? says the doctor, and she says, You mean you can fix me? The doctor pulls from a drawer a shotgun and says, Good news.

Eddy grows bigger through some black magic of his.

Some people, Esther says, enjoy what is called a sense of humor. My sister for one. She could teach you about it.

In the room behind them other men dwindle and conduct interior lives and chew foods rounded and brined to fleshy, to brainy, to eyeball consistency.

Actually the woman is not ugly, just plain—I told it wrong, Esther says. And the doctor, he says nothing. He just flat out shoots.

Don't hog a conversation, Esther says when she cannot bear it.

Eddy holds out his hand. Calm down, he says. I want my reading cold.

Yes, that's right, no talking and no touch either, Esther says. That's stage one. That's by the book. Sight only. That's the only way to do it if you want it done right.

Hush, Eddy says and opens.

The last night Doris visits Muddy River is not hot but cold. Freak snow in June. A light rain falls, curdles, lazes to a float. Each gas lamp an astonishing aquarium of flakes. Ice hangs her lashes and gums the drum leak and sheathes the sedge grass that cracks loud beneath her. The season gone bad. She must harvest her take. But when Doris reaches beneath the dock to her safekeeping ledge she finds just slime. Numb fingers fumble, find only limpets. Muddy

River would not take what is hers without a return—it pays up square, she counts on this—so she pinches her nose against the stink and scrambles down the bank. In waist-high muck she hunts one-handed. Under the dock is a reeking dark cave. Moss scuttles her scalp. She can see little in this light beyond her own hand patting the scum for bottles. Her own hand shattering frozen sedge grass. Foot by foot through the cold suck of mudbed. By the last dock post, her hand closes on something. Not bottle. Flesh.

Perhaps she screams.

Next thing she observes is herself on the dock in a violent foot-to-skull shiver. The sky powdered with stars.

That is when Muddy River grows verbal.

Look again, it says. I have what I owe you.

Once more, she finds her way down the bank, through mud, under dock, to the post. There awaits Deacon in the body of a small man faceup afloat. His flesh is quite blue—no clothes whatsoever. Four bruises trace a line where her stones had struck: single file from foot to hip. Beyond this, he looks wholly serviceable. Doris drags him to shore and clutches him to her to warm him. His face in repose is appropriate. The right human house. She rubs the rough blue cheeks in circles. Sluggard blood moves, animates the fingers. They turn a fine pink. Then the small good hand encloses her wrist. She knows its touch.

Deacon has come home to her for good. He can free Esther of Doris. She has paid for him and he is hers to keep.

The day Doris and Esther left for Boston, all the front doors of Holyoke failed to close. They sagged and could not clear their jambs. The doors had sent word, one to the other, and it was agreed: Not a thing goes uncounted. Not one stolen screw.

ACKNOWLEDGMENTS

This book would not exist without the support of my teachers, Michelle Latiolais, Ron Carlson, Christine Schutt, Richard Godden, Michael Ryan, and Jim McMichael; the faith of the academic Frankensteins, Nicole, Nadya, Sneza, and Angela; the beneficence of friends and readers, Brad, Nell, Annie, Emily, Alan, Matt, Ryan, and Janice; the magnificence of Maji; the wit of the Wilding; and the good humor of my family. Special thanks to Mike Levine, who saw a book, and to Nasser, who feeds me.